J

Rebel
Cargo

SEP 08

CH

For Beaula

First published in Great Britain in 2007 by
Frances Lincoln Children's Books, 4 Torriano Mews,
Torriano Avenue, London NW5 2RZ
www.franceslincoln.com

First paperback edition 2007

British Library Cataloguing in Publication Data
available on request

ISBN: 978-1-84507-525-5

Set in Plantin

Printed and bound in Great Britain
by Mackays of Chatham

1 3 5 7 9 8 6 4 2

Rebel Cargo

James Riordan

Foreword by
Beaula Kay McCalla

F
FRANCES LINCOLN
CHILDREN'S BOOKS

Foreword

My eyes widened as I read each word, each page. At first the characters were detached from me. I made them so. I did not want to feel the pain: to empathise was enough. No one, no book was going to tell me how I should feel.

I didn't have to wait long. Things started to come together for me when Abena was described as having a 'lucky' gap in her front teeth. The same as mine.

She looked like me. She shared a history with me. Was it all coincidence?

'And eventually… some children of children of children did return to see their ancestral homes again' – now this story really was about me!

'Eventually' – for me that was some four or five hundred years later.

Some went back to step in the footprints left in the dusty caves of the holding ports. Some went back to reclaim a family name, a custom, a tribe. I went back to my ancestral home, my motherland of Bioko, in Equatorial Guinea, in the Bight of Biafra. The lost daughter had returned, the day had arrived; it was written in the stars. The sun shone down on the sleepy countryside and, as I walked towards my village, it came alive with gentle drumming and singing. I was greeted with amazement and wonder. *Who is she? Where did she come from? Who did she say she was?*

I looked into the eyes of my blood relative and hugged her so tightly! She wiped away my tears. I physically touched one of those who never left, one who was never stolen, raped or tortured.

I reclaimed my family name: Musodji. I was given a fantastic homecoming ceremony that I shall never forget. I simply went back to get what was mine, my identity: *sankofa* – a Ghanaian word symbolising the need to return to and know one's past in order to be able to move forward.

All this was made possible through DNA research, in 2002. When I donated a few of my cheek cells, I never dreamed that they would hold so much detail.

Now I can completely understand Abena's survival, for I am a result of her resilience and hope. Because of her, and many like her who fought to see Africa again, to be free, I can never forget what they went through.

To the future, to my children's children and their children, to the past, to my grandma and to all our mothers, I say: *Nele le* – the Bubi tribe's way of saying 'I am well', we survived.

B. M'Calla Lasakero

Bristol, October 2004

One

Wrapping the grey muffler round his neck, Mungo stepped into the damp November night. It was just after midnight and the low growl of approaching thunder made him quicken his step. He didn't want to be caught in the coming storm.

As he rounded Tally Point, lightning cut a jagged gash across the heavens. For a split second it wreathed the pirate in a deathly glow.

Mungo shuddered.

Yet he couldn't help stealing a fearful glance at the figure standing upright in his iron cage. He was staring at the boy through empty eye wells. Just then, a second flash of lightning lit up the grinning skull.

Mungo covered his eyes.

Bodies of pirate captains were as regular as the tides at Tally Point, a warning to all land and sea-lubbers. Tarred from top to toe to preserve the rotting flesh, they were strung up in chains and bound by iron hoops – as if the Devil might come to claim his own.

BY KING'S ORDER
THEIR TOES SHALL DANGLE
ABOVE THE LOW WATER MARK
UNTIL THREE TIDES WASH OVER THEM

But Billy Bones's blackened corpse had hung there for as long as Mungo could remember, since 1720 for sure. Crowds still came to stare at the grisly remains before trooping into Spice Island Inn to steady their nerves.

Mungo shivered with cold and fear. The gruesome body drew his gaze like a magnet. Crows had long since pecked out the eyes and now the shadowy sockets seemed to dog his every step. Jagged white teeth gleamed inside the black skull, as if mocking his fear.

Rain had freshened up the remains, and the stench clung to Mungo's damp skin and clothes.

Alongside the iron cage stood the scaffold, awaiting its next batch of brigands. It flung out a rigid arm against the sky, like the finger of Doom pointing to the gates of Hell. *Abandon hope, all ye who enter here!* it seemed to say.

Only that morning an entire pirate crew had swung on the hangman's rope – to cheers and jeers from a gawking mob. Amid the babble at the inn, Mungo had heard a gin-flushed woman screech out, 'Did you see that wee cabin boy bawling his eyes out? The noose soon had him choking on his sins! Good riddance to 'em all, I say! Good riddance to 'em all!'

The crowd cheered and chorused, 'Good riddance to 'em all! 'Good riddance to 'em all!'

Mungo pulled the frayed jacket collar up to his ears and hurried on, as slanting rain pricked his face.

Two

Mungo Mullins hadn't always been a homeless waif. He'd grown up in a small house in the shadow of the tall red-brick wall that stretched for miles around the boat-building yards of Portsea.

His father was always saying the house was made to measure, like an officer's bespoke uniform. It was tall enough for wooden stairs to three floors, yet narrow enough to touch both walls with outstretched arms.

The tall, thin house of the tall, thin man was a lively place of an evening when Dad had his friends in. Like himself, they were mostly whiskery seafaring captains with many a tale to tell, a shanty to sing and a taste for Mr Jeffs' fine ales. Often, little Mungo would be hoisted on to the parlour table to dance a jig to fiddle and concertina, or to sing a song his mother had taught him. Bleary-eyed and happy, he'd be hauled off to his attic cot – to dream of ghostly galleons sailing out of the mist, of desert islands where pirate gold was buried, and of cutthroat pirates like Blackbeard: 'a cutlass in each hand, six pistols slung across his chest and slow-burning fuses above his ears, so that his entire shaggy head seemed on fire as he went into battle' – such was the portrait painted by a captain who'd crossed cutlasses with him.

Home contained a fair sprinkling of Mungo's mother too. The neat rows of books on parlour shelves, the darkly polished oak dresser and table, the sweet smell of freshly scattered sawdust on the scullery floor, the daily-scrubbed doorstep, the lamp-blacked cooking stove and copper boiler – and the home always shipshape and Bristol fashion, as befitted a parson's daughter and captain's wife.

Mungo's father had gone to sea as a young lad and worked his way up from cabin boy to captain, spending nearly on thirty years before the mast. He ended up master of his own sailing ship, a two-masted, square-rigged brig that did the rum and spice run across the Atlantic to Cuba and Jamaica. It had been a profitable business – until, one day, pirates raided the brig and sent her to Davy Jones's Locker. Only three of the crew survived, picked up by a passing merchantman.

After his brush with pirates, Mungo's father came ashore, settled down as tutor to naval officers' children and took a wife. By now he was grizzled and weather-beaten, coming up for fifty – 'too old for the sea and too young for the land', he used to say. Yet he never seemed to find his land legs. Even after Mungo's birth, the lure of the sea made him restless. And when an old sailing companion invited him to join his crew as first mate, he jumped at the opportunity. It was a light sailing sloop, taking settlers over to America to start life anew in the New World.

With women and children on board, the sloop's master suggested Mungo's father bring his wife along as nurse and midwife – after all, the voyage was likely to last a good fifty or sixty days. Mungo's mother readily agreed, if only to keep her husband off the rum.

But there was a more pressing reason for them to abandon their six-year old son for six months. Mungo's father was deep in debt. Apart from the loss of his brig and valuable cargo, he owed money on the house and unpaid ale bills. The brewer, Mr Jeffs, had extended his payment deadline time and again, but he was now calling in the debt. The money they'd earn as first mate and sick nurse would clear the debts and enable the family to start life afresh, perhaps in America, if they liked what they saw.

Mungo was left in the care of an old widow woman – 'Old Missus Vinegar' he called her – who moved into the family home. The night the sloop sailed out on the tide, he cried his eyes out: he couldn't bear the thought of not seeing his parents for so long. No more merry musical evenings. No more colourful sea stories. No more bedtimes being tucked up by Mum. No more tender hugs and kisses – at least, not until the following spring.

Little did Mungo know that spring would never come.

Almost as soon as the sloop sailed through the harbour mouth, an unexpected squall blew up in the Solent. The sailing ship managed to navigate the Isle of Wight, but a powerful gust of wind dashed the little craft down on the Needles rocks. All hands and passengers went down with the ship.

Mungo only heard of the tragedy much later. Old Missus Vinegar decided he was too young to bear the loss. It was only when the boy was walking down Queen Street one morning, fetching lamp-black from the ironmonger's, that he learned the truth. He bumped into an old sea-dog drinking companion of his father's.

'Right sorry I am, little Mungie,' the man said, head bowed.

Alarm bells started to ring in Mungo's head.

'What about?' he said, hand over mouth.

The man turned turkey-red and tried to hurry on. But Mungo wouldn't let him go.

'Stop!' he yelled. 'Tell me!'

His hands shaking, the grey-bearded captain pulled the little lad to him, tears brimming in his eyes.

'Sorry, matey,' he murmured. 'I thought you knew about your mum and dad.'

'Are they dead?'

'Drowned. Off the Needles. Right sorry I am, lad. If there's anything...'

His voice tailed off in the distance as Mungo rushed home to bury his face in the feather bolster.

He had no one now. His grandparents were dead.

His mother and father were gone. He was all alone in the world.

The house would be sold to pay off the debts. Where would he go? What would he do? How would he survive?

To add to his problems, he came downstairs to find a note pinned to the dresser shelf. It was from Missus Vinegar.

Mungo,

> *Judging from thee crying, Thou knowest.*
> *It's best out.*
> *My task's done.*
> *God Bless Thee.*

> *Widow Birdson*

The next few weeks passed in a blur. House and contents were disposed of and Mungo found himself on the street. Of a daytime, he sometimes made a few farthings and halfpennies mud-larking – scrabbling for coins that passers-by tossed into The Hard's stinking mud uncovered by the ebb. Even though he washed in the incoming tide, the cloying stench lingered on. But scrapping for coins with other starving scallywags toughened him up and prepared him for a string of part-time jobs done for a crust of bread.

From the time he was orphaned, Mungo toiled like a galley-slave, scrubbing floors and tables, salting and gutting fish, sewing fishing nets, shifting tea-chests, unloading heavy sacks of sugar and spice. He'd put his hand to anything to survive.

To look at him, you'd think a gust of wind would snatch him up like thistledown and whisk him out to sea. He was nothing but skin and gristle – tough and wiry, though, like twisted hemp, and as bright as a button. He needed his wits about him to keep body and soul together. As Jonah Feltham, the innkeeper, used to say, 'Mungo's as tough as old sea-boots.'

It was his willingness to work hard that got him a job as skivvy at Spice Island Inn. He received no money; instead, Mr Feltham let him scavenge whatever crumbs of bread and cheese got swept up from the floor, plus a little extra if he felt in the mood – which wasn't often.

At about the same time, whether from a twinge of conscience or natural kindness, Mr Jeffs the brewer let Mungo doss down in his stables. The 'snug' was just a pile of sacks and straw in a lean-to at the end of Priddy's Yard. Though it was stifling hot in summer and perishing cold in winter, it mostly kept out the salty spray and bitter wind. Mungo repaid the debt by feeding and mucking out the brewer's two drays, Bessie and Josh.

All three enjoyed the company. Mungo would tell them the news of the day, read stories and share with them his hopes and dreams. And the horses would cock an ear and give a sympathetic grunt or whinny.

The worst thing about the stable was the rats – hordes of them. The hungry devils crept out at night, sniffing toes and ears, and trampling over Mungo's chest. Not that they found any tasty morsels on his skinny frame. In any case, he was so tired after a hard day's work that roaring lions wouldn't have disturbed his dreams. One day, for sure, someone would find his bones picked clean!

But he had no choice. It was either the stable or the workhouse.

Beggars can't be choosers.

Three

Mungo's mother had taught him to read and write. So he was able to earn himself a few groats reading letters to sailors at the inn, even penning replies to loved ones far away.

Whenever he could, he borrowed dusty books from the inn shelves. Mr Feltham didn't mind, as long as Mungo brought them back dusted clean and with no dog-ears on the pages. They were mostly about the sea and ships, expeditions to the New World and the Spanish Main, Admiralty Reports, tales of England's heroes who'd singed the beards of Dutchies, Frenchmen or Spaniards. There was nothing Mungo loved more than to snuggle down with a book and sail away to the South Seas, bask in the tropical sun and dig up buried treasure.

While Mungo's dreams shed shafts of sunbeams into his life, work at the inn was unending gloom. The regulars treated him as they would a stray dog, tossing him scraps of cheese and sausage-rind, splashing ale over the floor he'd just scrubbed, cursing and kicking him if he got under their feet. With his pinched red face, turned-up nose, spiky ginger hair and skin chapped by sea spray, the regulars took him for a land urchin, a ragamuffin, Cabin Boy of the Good Ship Spice Island. And cabin boys were the dregs of the rum barrel, the lowest rung of the ladder, apprentice Jack Tars who had to be pummelled into shape like dough.

Mungo bore his wretched life with quiet determination. He was alive, that was enough. And if he could get through another day without broken bones, gulp down enough food to stave off hunger, that would take care of his bodily needs.

As for the mind – well, he read and watched and listened. Words were like grains of gold. As he shuffled over the spit-and-sawdust floor, clearing away the empties, he always lent an ear to the colourful yarns.

And what a crew of storytellers they were! Men who'd sailed the seven seas, swigged rum with wily seadogs like Francis Drake and Jack Hawkins; men with one eye, one leg or arm; men who'd made a fortune and drunk or gambled it away; men who had a tale to tell.

Take old Alex Selkirk, whose shipmates had marooned him on a desert island. Somehow he'd survived alone for nigh on twenty-five years. Now, blind and lame, when the firewater heated up his bones he'd tilt back his head and sing in a rum-sodden voice, first softly, as if to himself, then raising his voice to the rafters, flinging his words at the world:

'Oh, me name was Billy Bray when I sailed,
When I sailed,
Me name was Billy Bray when I sailed,
Me name was Billy Bray,
God's laws I did betray
And so wickedly did I pay, when I sailed.

Take warning now by me, for I must die,
I must die.
Take warning now by me
And shun bad company,
Lest you come to hell with me, for I die.'

As the song trailed away, the inn would fall silent. Lopsided grins would greet the shanty. And someone else would launch into a rambling tale of the sea.

One night, as Selkirk's shaky hand raised the pewter mug to his lips, a low throaty voice came from a dingy corner.

'Who can say who's a pirate, eh? Pirate or privateer, rogue or England's hero, it's all the same.'

When no one responded, the low voice continued, 'Raid Spanish ships and share the booty with the King and his lords – and they call you "sir" and "hero" – like those cut-throats Drake and Hawkins. But come back empty-handed, with no gold to line King William's pockets, and – SWISH! OFF WITH HIS HEAD!'

A few bold souls waggled their beards in agreement.

Some kept mum. But several flung out patriotic shouts: 'God Save King William!' 'Long Live the King!'

As for Mungo, he felt a thrill of excitement course through his veins. He admired bold talk and anyone who cut through the usual bravado. Who was this shadowy figure? He sounded foreign.

Little did Mungo know the man was to change his life – and Mungo his...

Four

The red-faced man was standing over her, feet planted either side of her body. Large hairy hands were reaching for her throat. Yellow eyeballs were filled with hatred, thick red lips were twisted in a snarl, a hooked nose sprouting red tufts of hair snorted like a bush-pig: *'Hoink-hoink!'*

'HELP! It's the White Man come to eat me! *Aiy-yee-eee-eee-eee!*

The girl's screams woke up her mother.

'Hush, Abena.'

She fell silent, occasional whimpers escaping from her throat. She was still in the clutches of the nightmare ogre, trembling all over, teeth chattering, body soaked in sweat, legs clammy where she'd wee'd herself.

Although Abena tried to conjure up happy, homely pictures, the red monster kept popping up, poking his ape-bum face round the corner of the long-drop door, spoiling games of hopscotch and knucklebones, jumping out from behind the trees.

Abena did her best to drive him away. In all her twelve years she'd never seen a white man close up. But outside the *barracoon* she'd overheard white talk –

a hard, squawking noise like early morning crows.

Now she was wide awake. Sleep wouldn't return, no matter how hard she tried. All her senses told her the nightmare was real. As she raised her head, she could see, in the half-dark, row upon row of black bodies lying on the muddy earth; their wrists and ankles were chained to bodies on either side.

She felt the steamy, stifling heat and the pain of chafed hands and feet from the iron chains that shackled her to her mother on one side, and to her elder sister Afi on the other.

The girl smelt the vomit and festering sores of hundreds of naked bodies inside the stone prison. Desperately, her nose tried to block out the overpowering sour, putrid stench of faeces.

She heard the cacophony of screams and groans, retching and praying – some of it in a language she didn't understand. The babble blended together with baying dogs, bawling guards and breaking surf beyond the rocky walls. She recalled her first glimpse of the sea: three parallel lines of green palms, brown sand and boiling white surf.

Abena could taste a thin, sour bile on her parched lips – all that was left in her empty belly.

From top to toe, her entire body was wracked with pain because of the beatings she'd suffered on the long trek – how many turns of the moon was it? She'd lost count. Her neck was stiff and sore from the leather thongs that had tied her to four others in the coffle as it shuffled down forest paths, floundered through deep streams, trotted over sun-baked plains.

There had been twenty prisoners to start with, five to a coffle: ten from her village added to the ten already yoked together. But they'd picked up another eighty on the way. Of the hundred, only half made it to the tide-water. A couple had deliberately eaten poisonous plants to kill themselves – but it only made them sick and earned a severe beating from the black slave dealers in charge.

Once, the party was attacked by a pack of hungry hyenas; one girl was bitten so badly, she was left for the lions to finish off. Crocodiles accounted for five others; yoked together, water up to their necks, the prisoners couldn't defend themselves; so when a crocodile grabbed the legs of one, it dragged down the other four.

Most died of hunger, thirst and exhaustion. Dying or dead, they were flung to lurking beasts.

On the way they passed the ruins of villages burned down in slave raids. It was eerie: no women singing as they pounded mealies; no chattering men hoeing neat rows of beans; no happy laughter of children as they played their games. Just deathly silence, broken only by the patter of wind-blown brush scuttling across the empty yards.

As memories seared her mind, fury and frustration

gripped Abena and she hit out angrily, jerking at the chains that bound her. At once she was sorry. Afi groaned, and on the other side her mother cried sharply, 'Abena!'

The girl fell back, uncoiling her tense body and sinking into the warm mire.

Why had Nyame, the great Sky God, sent such misfortune? One moment free, the next – a slave.

Five

Lying in the dark, Abena recalled her village: working alongside her sister, mother and grandmother: hoeing, planting, watering, grubbing, feeding the chickens and pounding ears of corn into mealy bran. Now and then she'd go hunting with other children for rabbit, bush-pig and ostrich – as well as killing pests like jackals, foxes and rats, and protecting their homes from deadly spiders, snakes and scorpions.

With her brother Kwame, she learned to gather wild honey from bees' nests in the hollows of trees and find sweet berries and roots to eat, to drink warm creamy milk from a goat's udder, to swim naked in fresh, clear streams and catch fish with twine and sharpened bits of wire.

In the village they shared everything as naturally as the air they breathed and the rain they drank. The goats and chickens belonged to everyone; their milk, meat and eggs went to those who needed them most – a sick child, a pregnant mother, a hungry infant. When she and Kwame brought home birds and fish, they went straight into the communal pot.

Best of all, Abena loved the evenings, when all the village would gather in the square beneath the big shady tree. In the centre squatted blind Kofi, his voice rusty in his throat, telling stories, passing on the proud history of his people. His voice would be high and low, soft and sly, loud and harsh as he mimicked different animals: the hiss of a snake, the roar of a lion, the chuckle of a hyena, the piping and cawing of birds.

He always began his story in the same way:

'Listen, my people, our stories have been handed down from our ancestors in the faraway time. You must tell them to your children, they will tell their children, and so on down the ages. They are our memory...'

Most of his stories told of a time when only animals roamed the earth: Anansi the spider, who could climb up to the skies on a spider thread and talk with Nyame the Sky God; Simba the lion, who was king of the animals; the river goddess Yemoya and her lovely daughter Aje who wed the handsome earth chief Oduduwe. In some tales there were lion women so beautiful that, when men fell in love with them, they ended up being eaten by their wives!

Story and music came together in the storyteller's telling. His beautiful songs could lift you up even as they told their sad story. You might be poor, but the song gave you hope; it reached down into every fibre of your body so that you couldn't help yourself: your whole body swayed to its rhythm.

Kofi's stories had an answer to every question – such as how people of different colours came into the world. One day the Sky God baked the first people out of clay. But he took out the first batch before they were done – so they came out pale and white like locusts. He left the second batch in the oven too long – so they got burned as black as ebony. The third, however, came out perfectly brown, like ripe dates.

This was why the Moors in the north were as black as night, the *backra* on the coast were locust white, while Abena's tribe, of course, was burnished golden brown... From the tales Abena learned important lessons: that Good always triumphs over Evil; that having brains is better than having brawn; that underdogs need infinite patience, stubbornness and unshakeable hope; that peace is better than war, cleverness than stupidity, love than hate, patience than hotheadedness. And forgiveness is better than revenge.

Some stories were set in the Ashanti lands which had once stretched from the Sahara Desert in the north to the River Niger in the east, all the way to the Atlantic Ocean. The king, or *oba,* could lead as many as two thousand soldiers into battle. So great was the capital city that it was surrounded by a six-mile, ten-foot-high wall. Shady trees lined the broad streets, and the houses were made of red clay polished like red marble. The *oba* lived in a vast palace with square galleries whose pillars were covered in bronzes showing the Ashanti's heroic deeds. They were a proud people whose empire had its own code of laws, great stone buildings and skilled workers in wood, brass and iron.

But a time had come when the kingdom fell into decline. From the north it was attacked by the Moors and, from the south, by savage tribes like the Fang – cannibals with sharp-filed teeth. Both raiders were encouraged by Europeans who, like sharks scenting blood, arrived in their ships and supplied both sides with muskets, gunpowder and lead gunshot. In exchange they demanded slaves.

Not only did the white men bring weapons to kill, they also brought a drug that dulled men's minds. And when the drug started to take hold, its price began to rise. Soon, in exchange for the white man's firewater, chiefs were willing to sell their own people as slaves, who would disappear beyond the seas, never to return. These slaves were fit men and women. The slavers weren't interested in the young or old: they only wanted the able-bodied. Some said that white men were cannibals with a taste for black flesh and that once they'd taken them to their own land, they built a great fire and roasted the black bodies on a spit.

Abena remembered that fateful day when the village medicine man received his first keg of rum from the white man's *caboceer*, Fat Sam. As Sam's cruel, beady eyes looked on, the medicine man summoned all the villagers together and announced that black magic was afoot. He'd heard strange noises on his roof at night... It was the *baloyi*, evil spirits who rode naked on the backs of baboons and sucked people's blood when they were asleep. There was only one thing to do: the medicine man would have to sniff out villagers who'd become servants of the *baloyi*. That was the only way to save the village.

Once the frightened villagers had been assembled on the square, the medicine man danced around them, sniffing loudly and pulling out the culprits: they included Abena and her family – her mother, father, sister and brother. She recalled with horror how her father had appealed to his neighbours not to listen to the medicine man, how the man was filled with greed for firewater. But many were scared – and relieved that they'd not been sniffed out themselves.

When no one listened, Abena's father had struck down the drunken medicine man with his fist. Right away a shot rang out: Fat Sam calmly shot him dead.

Then, with the survivors cowed by Fat Sam's magic fire-stick, the *baloyi*'s servants were yoked to a coffle and taken away. That was the last Abena saw of her home, friends and village.

She softly wept.

Six

It was with thoughts of pirates in his head that Mungo made his way home that night. He'd just passed the rotting pirate when the storm broke, and he bent his head into the gale. As he did so, his eyes caught a movement by the scaffold.

The blood froze in his veins.

Was it a rat? No, bigger.

A stray dog? No, bigger still.

There was something unnatural about it that made him avert his gaze, wishing it would go away. What was worse, he now caught snatches of half-groans, half-yelps – like an animal in pain.

A volley of vivid flashes lit up the scene as clear as day. At the foot of the scaffold steps cowered a slight figure, human, not animal. He could see it distinctly now.

It was a young boy dressed in baggy blue breeches and a grubby linen shirt. His hair was hidden by a bandanna. His feet were bare, his face was buried in his hands, and he was sobbing as if his heart would break.

Most surprising of all was his skin. It was black, as black as the pitch slapped on a ship's hull. Mungo had heard of black people from a crew serving on slavers that had sailed to Africa; but he'd never seen one with his own eyes.

As Mungo approached, the black boy jerked up his head and gazed wildly at him, shrinking into the shadows. Mungo tried to calm him:

'Who-aah. Steady, lad, steady,' he murmured. 'Easy does it, easy. I won't hurt you. Trust me.'

He edged forward as he spoke, holding out his hand, as if the boy were a nervous puppy who needed to sniff his fingers.

The boy must have seen that Mungo was scarcely older than himself. Gradually his groans died away to snuffles, his heaving shoulders quivered once, twice, and were still. He leaned back with a ragged sigh against the bottom step, staring forlornly at Mungo. In the glimmer of the moon Mungo saw that his face was desperately miserable.

'You can't stay here, matey,' he said. 'You'll freeze to death. Come, I'll take you to the inn. Maybe they'll give you food and shelter.'

'No, no, no!' the boy suddenly screamed, and the wild look reappeared in his eyes.

Mungo didn't know what to say.

'Well, let me help you home,' he said.

The boy was silent for a while, every so often darting wary glances at Mungo. With a despairing cry, he pointed to the sea. Then he bent forward with a groan, shoulders hunched, face hidden in his hands.

Mungo made up his mind.

'Look, come back with me if you like. It's only a stable full of straw and old rags. But it's dry and warm, and no one'll bother you.'

Unsteadily, the barefoot boy got to his feet; he almost fainted with the effort. Mungo darted forward and caught him by the arm. How cold he was! Through the thin shirt his flesh was as cold as death. Leaning on Mungo for support, he stumbled along the quay, groaning with every step. Mungo led him over a footbridge and past the dark walls of the boatyard. There was little he could do to protect the boy from the driving rain. They were both drenched to the skin and shivering. But at last they reached the dingy shack.

Pushing open the door, Mungo helped the boy inside. It was all suddenly so dry and silent. With a scared look, the boy collapsed on a pile of straw.

The grumpy mare whinnied sleepily in one corner. Lighting a candle stub upon the window ledge, Mungo got a better view of the homeless stray.

He lay back exhausted on the straw, arms akimbo, black strands of hair tumbling about his shoulders. His face was at once childish in its innocence and world-weary in its agelessness – like a little old man with features etched by wind and woe. Although he was dressed shabbily in faded shirt and breeches, for the first time Mungo noticed a bright red sash about his neck, and a brass earring. Steam was beginning to rise from his damp clothes.

'You can stay here as long as you like,' Mungo said quietly. 'Maybe I can find you work at the inn.'

For a moment he thought the boy had fallen asleep. But his eyes flickered open. Mungo stuck out his hand awkwardly, as if to seal the bargain. The boy made a wan effort at a smile, grasping the hand with ice-cold fingers, black on white.

Then he fell back and was soon sleeping soundly.

Throwing a couple of dry sacks over the boy's rain-sodden body, Mungo crept to the far corner of the barn. There he lay down wearily on a bed of straw and was soon fast asleep.

Company added comfort to his dreams.

Seven

Early next morning, Mungo rose with the watery dawn and tiptoed over to his newfound friend. He was lying in the same position as the night before. But all trace of pain had gone from his face; it was as if a hot iron had smoothed out the wrinkles.

He looked as peaceful as an angel. Mungo smiled down at the sleeping form.

'Sleep on, bonny lad, sleep on,' he murmured.

His presence made Mungo feel good. He imagined how cheery life would be when the boy was fit and well. They could tell each other stories. They could go exploring together. They could dig up buried treasure, sail away on a clipper – Mungo as Captain, the boy as first mate.

His head bursting with plans, he cleaned out the stalls, fed the horses and shoved handfuls of fresh straw beneath their feet while they munched and clumped. He shared the pail of fresh water with the two drays, first washing his own face in the bucket before splashing water into the wooden trough. The horses didn't seem to mind Mungo's sleepy dust in their drinking water.

This morning he gave himself more of a lick and

promise than a proper wash. He was keen to get some food down the sickly lad. As soon as he could, he ran to the inn for the usual breakfast scraps: tacky biscuits, some cheese and sausage, and a mug of hot water.

The new day was crisp and clear, and the streaky sky shed no more tears. Rain still glistened on the cobblestones, but Billy Bones was not as scary as the night before.

Once back at the stable, Mungo put the food down on the hay-strewn floor, then shook the boy gently. 'Come on, matey. Wakey, wakey. Drink up while the water's hot.'

The arm he shook was icy cold.

He shook him more firmly. The body seemed oddly stiff, like half-frozen rags.

Blind panic seized Mungo.

He slid one hand beneath the boy's shirt to feel his heart. No sign of life at all!

As he withdrew his fingers, they hooked on to something. It was a scrap of paper. But he hardly gave it a second glance. Now was not the time to pry into people's secrets. Thrusting it down his own shirt, he cried, 'Oh my God! He's gone and croaked on me!'

There was no time to lose. Perhaps it was not too late…

He rushed for help.

As luck would have it, he bumped straight into the hangman on his way to the inn.

'Come quickly,' Mungo cried. 'I think my friend's gone and died.'

'If you mean the pirate,' said the red-faced man, 'he's been as dead as a doornail for goin' on two year.'

'No, no,' Mungo cried. 'The black lad from the scaffold.'

At the word 'scaffold', the man stopped in his tracks. With a sigh, he forced all thought of breakfast from his mind and reluctantly followed Mungo to the stable.

Eight

Mungo watched, ashen-faced, as the man bent over the body, feeling the pulse and listening for a breath or heart-beat.

All at once, he leapt back as if stung by a wasp.

'Holy sharks!' he exclaimed. 'What the devil's *he* doing here?'

Mungo didn't understand. What was the man talking about?

'Do you know him, then?'

'Know him?' the hangman squawked. 'I darn well ought to... I hanged him myself yesterday morning!' He was staring goggle-eyed at the boy, muttering, 'It's a ghost. It *must* be a ghost!'

'You can't have hanged him,' cried Mungo. 'He was alive last night. I spoke to him. He spoke to me... We shook hands.'

But the man went on firing words aimlessly into the air. 'Off a pirate ship... red-handed... whole caboodle... tried, sentenced, hanged... Good job too. I strung 'em up... every man jack of them! I'd remember a black face, sure enough – like a black gull among the herrings.' Perhaps he feared for his job. If it got out that he'd let a prisoner escape the noose, there'd be hell to pay. He could lose his baccy and rum perks. So he stuck to his guns: the boy was a ghost, come back to haunt him...

Mungo remembered the officer coming to the inn for a pint of porter at midday. He'd boasted of stringing up a crew of cut-throats, including the black cabin boy who'd squirmed and kicked at the end of the rope.

'While you were at the inn,' he said, 'maybe the rope slipped off his skinny neck and he fell to the ground. Either he fainted, or he lay there hiding behind the scaffold till I found him.'

But the hangman wouldn't have it. As he hurried off to fetch help – to toss the body into the sea before the story got out – Mungo knelt down and undid the red sash from the dead boy's throat. Freed from the sash, the head flopped backwards at an unnatural angle. Mungo stared. There were red welts on the neck – from the hangman's rope! And on the right side of his chest there was something else: an ugly red scar tinged with purple. The letters 'SV' were clearly branded on it. Who could have done such a cruel thing!

The boy was no ghost. But who was he? What was a black boy doing on a white pirate ship? What had put an end to his short life?

While the hangman disposed of the body, Mungo set out to discover the lad's story.

Nine

Abena awoke to thunder: a single thunderbolt that echoed dully above her head. Then another, and another. Seven bolts in all. The thunder was followed by the weirdest sound she'd ever heard: a caterwauling like a herd of trumpeting elephants.

Something was happening. She could hear a babble of voices, pounding feet and urgent hammering as if stalls or tents were being erected on market day. All at once, the doors flew open and she had to shield her eyes from the sudden glare.

A giant of a man with long hair and beard, pock-marked brow, sunken cheeks and red face was bawling like a grumpy gorilla. Though she couldn't understand the words, their meaning was clear enough. With one hand he cracked a rawhide whip over the nearest row of bodies; with the other he pinched his nose against the vile stench that hit him in the face. Chains clanked, bodies stirred and helping hands pulled neighbours to their feet. Some were unable to rise: they would never rise again.

Since Abena had lain in the darkness for time out of mind, there was no way of telling how many moons had passed or whether it was night or day. To gorilla hoots of *'Oot, oot, oot!'*, columns of the living dead filed through the doorway into bright sunlight, leaving behind the dead and dying still shackled to their neighbours. It must have been around midday, for the fiery sun hung directly above their heads.

The slaves were herded down the sandy beach and instructed to wash in the sea. The sight of circling shark fins beyond the breakers was enough to deter any thought of striking out to sea and round the coast. Abena, Afi and Kwame did their best to cleanse their bodies of the cloying filth in the foaming surf, before helping their mother who was having trouble standing up – each successive wave knocked her back down again.

As her eyes grew accustomed to the light, Abena stole a glance about her. Ranged in a semi-circle before the rock face was a host of slaves – more than the eye could count. Some were standing, some sitting on the sand and shingle. Most were miserable, skinny skeletons with utterly dejected looks upon their faces. Some already had the stamp of death printed on them.

Within the semi-circle were half a dozen red-faced men talking together as they eyed up their black captives – for all the world assessing them as farmers would cattle at a fair.

Set apart from the mass were a dozen or so young girls, most about Abena's age. Their skins glistened with palm oil, their ears, necks and wrists were hung with fine jewellery, their hair was carefully brushed, combed and oiled. Barely a yard of cloth encircled their hips, and even that was being torn away by dealers as the red-faced ones poked and prodded.

Abena's eyes were drawn to the most extraordinary sight of all. Beneath a great flame banyan tree with roots like elephant feet was a black man, squatting on a gnarled tree root. His ample figure was clothed in a scarlet coat laced with rusty gold and silver; on his head was a tall black top hat minus its lid. His feet were bare.

Abena guessed this was some local king who claimed ownership of the slaves, and that he'd come to receive his due. The caterwauling had come from elephant-teeth trumpets that hung at the sides of a dozen attendants. The thunderbolt salute had been provided by a cannon from the clipper riding in the bay.

Abena realised that the white man must be the King of the Sea. But beyond the trees lay the realm of the black chief and others like him. Despite their fire-power, few whites dared venture into the forest for fear of fever, snakes, mosquitoes and hostile Africans. As for the sandy strip between sea and forest, that was no-man's land, reserved for bargaining and housing slaves.

While the inmates of the *barracoon* were being beaten by sticks and 'tickled' with the cat-o'-nine-tails towards the outer rows of the semi-circle, bodies were being dragged out and deposited like jetsam on the beach as a meal for hungry dogs and for the tide to wash out to the waiting sharks.

When all the slaves were settled, the ceremony commenced. At a signal from the shore, the guns boomed and trumpets blasted the air. That was the cue for the long-haired Captain in navy-blue uniform and shiny peaked cap to lead a line of red men in striped shirts to present gifts to the man the Captain addressed as 'Drunken Lord Willoughby'. No one overstepped the fringes of the banyan shade out of respect for this god-like personage.

Set on the ground before Drunken Lord Willoughby were trays containing strings of beads, ten brass rings, four copper bars and rolls of cotton cloth. All the while, an attendant at his elbow filled and refilled a cup from a keg of rum.

Once the gifts had been presented, the bargaining began. Since neither side spoke the other's language, the barter was done by means of hand signals, shrugs, pursed lips and waving arms..

Not all the slaves belonged to the chief. By tradition, however, the royal slaves had to be sold off first and at a higher price, irrespective of sex, age or fitness.

The first lot to be led out was a group of six strapping youths – clearly the best of the bunch and the most prized. Before the bidding could start, the

Captain beckoned forward another officer, evidently the ship's surgeon, who carefully examined the young men, ensuring they were sound of wind and limb. He peered into their mouths – presumably to gauge their age by counting teeth; then he made them jump and stretch their arms, to search for lice or signs of clap or pox.

Only when the medical man was satisfied did he nod to his Captain, and an array of trading goods was produced from large wooden chests: muskets, kegs of gunpowder, knives, flints, silk handkerchiefs and brass pans and kettles.

The king drove a hard bargain. But the bearded Captain had learned to be patient, firm and diplomatic, observing all the royal niceties. He knew that once the strongest slaves were accounted for, the price would come down. Eventually a price was struck: all the goods on display plus five brass kettles per slave.

Ten

The second lot to be led out was the group of pretty young girls done up in their finery. Whereas the youths had stared insolently at the traders, the girls at first tried to smile sweetly as they had been ordered, but smiles soon gave way to tears as they were shamelessly examined by the ship's surgeon. The youngest-looking was discarded – perhaps because her unformed body made her useless for the purpose for which she was being sold, or perhaps because she was under four feet four inches – the minimum agreed height for slaves. She was sent to the back of the semi-circle, beside Abena's family.

Once again the dealers barked and haggled long and loudly before reaching agreement.

The third lot was a group of able-bodied men in their twenties and thirties. They were followed by worn-out, emaciated men and women, their heads shaven to conceal grey hair. Lastly came a sickly bunch of mixed-age women, their heads drooping from fatigue.

The tribute paid was made up of cutlasses and various items of clothing: hats, linen handkerchiefs, canvas trousers and calico shirts.

Just one last task remained before the bargain could be sealed. There and then the purchased slaves had to be branded with their new owner's mark. As the haggling came to an end, a couple of long-haired men in blue-and-white striped shirts, long canvas trousers and broad-brimmed hats started a log fire upon the sand. Into the hottest part of the flames they thrust long iron rods until the tips were red-hot.

One by one the slaves were brought forward and forced to kneel on the ground as a sailor pressed into their chests the sizzling brand with the initials of the ship: *SV* – *Sea Venture*. To Abena's amazement, the six youths showed no fear and boldly thrust out their chests to receive the red-hot irons. Not a flicker of pain crossed their faces.

'Those are Comorantine boys,' whispered the young girl next to Abena. 'Fanti and Ashanti; they're very brave. Not like the Ibo, who always scream like babies.'

Abena guessed the girl must be Fanti or Ashanti herself.

When it came to the young girls, who were to be branded on their right shoulders, a great howling and shrieking arose; most had to be gripped round the neck by one sailor, while another stamped the brand on to their flesh.

Once the branding was over and the marked slaves had been left to their agony, many groaning in excruciating pain, the entertainment began. Mostly, this consisted of eating and drinking in full view of the starving slaves. The smell of roast pig wafted beneath Abena's nostrils and turned her empty stomach over. Enviously she watched as Drunken Lord Willoughby and his white clients tossed meaty bones to the lurking pye-dogs, who fought over every scrap. The men washed down their food with tankards of beer, bowls of punch and drams of rum or brandy. These were accompanied by toasts proposed by the ship's Captain.

Each time he would get to his feet, sway in the breeze, brandish his pint mug and make a loud speech, raising his mug aloft and spilling much of the contents down his beard. If the words were insulting – 'you ignorant black pig!' – the listening king was none the wiser. He just grinned from ear to ear, nodding in agreement at the smiling Captain, sometimes repeating the word '*peeg*' and jabbing his stomach.

After several toasts, it was time for what the Captain called 'a spot of sport'.

A fat, bearded fellow was thrust forward from a small, wooden cell like a low chicken coop amidst the trees. The man was barely recognisable as white, black or brown, with his torn, dirty clothes and battered face. He turned out to be a Portuguese captain, also a slaver, captured by the English. They were about to introduce him to 'English sport'.

As the man was dragged across the ground to the English Captain, he clasped his hands together,

44

begging for his life. But the Captain just laughed and beckoned to a crew member to begin the 'fun'.

The man was pulled by his hair to the centre of the clearing; he was then tied with cords and hung from four stakes so that his entire weight was held by his thumbs and toes. While he screamed in agony, the sailor put heavy rocks on his stomach and burning palm leaves on his face until all his beard and skin were burned off. The king and Captain guffawed loudly, drunk on the brutal sport – well aware that each would do the same to the other, given half a chance.

More followed. Portuguese seamen were brought forward and stretched on a rack until their arms and legs cracked. Others had burning fuses stuck between their toes and fingers. One man, a priest judging by his dress, had a cord twisted so tightly about his head that his eyes popped out.

This was too much for Abena. As the party grew wilder and wilder, and the king and Captain grew more drunk, she shut her eyes and turned away.

Eleven

Later that afternoon, the purchased slaves were put into canoes and rowed to the ship's long-boat waiting beyond the surf and breakers. Abena watched them go, knowing she would soon follow. All at once she saw two of the shackled Comorantine boys stand up in the narrow canoe and dive overboard. Whether or not they intended to swim to safety she couldn't tell, but the sudden excitement of the circling sharks and the disappearance of the men beneath the waves told her the worst.

Would she be brave enough to thwart the slavers?

Abena's party was herded back into the *barracoon* and, next day, the same process of haggling was repeated.

Fat Sam conducted negotiations with the ship's Captain – without sweeteners of gifts, rum or inflated prices. This was strictly business. Whoever was not redeemed by family or friends was sold for a mixture of cowrie shells and brass neptunes or *basons* – the latter being large, thin, flat coins which could be cut into pieces and used to make bracelets and necklaces.

Abena, her sister and their mother were sold off in

one lot for a hundred strings of cowries, forty shells to a string. Kwame went for five strings of cowries, ten bars of iron, a roll of tobacco and a pipe of rum.

By no means all the slaves were sold. Some, the miserable *mackrons* were rejected at the medical examination – for bad teeth or eyes, grey hair or disease. They were left to make their own way home, or to fall prey to wild animals in the forest.

It was impossible for Abena not to shriek out when she felt the red-hot iron pressed into her flesh. It was agonising for weeks afterwards. But anyone making too much fuss had pepper or salt rubbed into the red-raw wound by hard-faced sailors. For many, worse was to come when they were marched down to the beach. Apart from their earlier midday dip, hardly anyone had seen the sea before. The youngsters especially were terrified, convinced that the sound of the surf was the roaring of some great sea-beast.

The stiffening breeze was sending mountains of white-crested breakers crashing on to the shore. If it hadn't been for the cat-o'-nine-tails and hippo-hide whips wielded by sailors and *caboceers*, no one would have boarded the seventy-foot canoes. Each canoe was paddled by twenty men and held eighty slaves; if a canoe capsized, both slaves and crew would be food for sharks. The beautiful white 'shells' visible through the clear water were in fact human bones picked clean.

As dusk fell, Abena found herself climbing a rope

ladder on to the ship that was to be her home for many moons.

Rumour had it, they were being taken across the ocean and sold to a race of giants called Koomi.

Twelve

Mungo scrubbed the plank floor of the inn parlour before sprinkling it with fresh wood shavings. Then he squatted in a corner, out of the way of early sippers and swiggers, and chewed on a sausage rind, squeezing out the juice. As he ate, he reflected on his short-lived friendship.

How had the black lad fallen in with pirates?

As he sat musing over the boy's fate, he suddenly remembered the scrap of paper. Did it hold some clue to the boy's fate?

Fumbling inside the threadbare shirt, his cold fingers reached the parchment lying, stiff and warm, below his rib cage. Gingerly he drew the paper out, trying not to tear it. Then he laid it carefully in his lap, smoothed out the crumpled edges and stared hard.

Disappointment. It contained no clue to the boy's tragic end. All the paper showed was a crude sketch. It showed two things. One was a sailing ship, maybe a barque or a clipper.

He knew his ships. It had a rear mast rigged fore and aft, along with a two square rigged mast – that almost certainly meant a clipper.

The second drawing was very odd: it looked like a ship sliced in half, with countless matchstick figures neatly drawn all the way round.

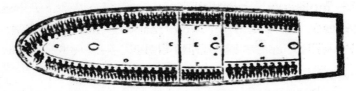

What on earth was it meant to be? There were five letters scrawled at the bottom, as if the artist couldn't write, but had copied them:

$$A B \mathcal{E} \eta A$$

Probably this was the ship's name. But what was so special about the ship and her name? And why was the paper hidden in the boy's shirt?

His thoughts were shattered by Mr Feltham's foghorn voice.

'Scoff my grub and scrub 'er clean! Get moving, you scurvy ratbag, or it's the press gang for you!'

Mungo was always hearing about men being clobbered on the head and dragged aboard a merchantman, or unwary drinkers sleeping it off in some alleyway, only to wake up at sea. That's how the

King's Navy gained most of its recruits.

Maybe that's how the boy had gone to sea. Perhaps they had sent the press gang to Africa!

Mungo scrambled to his feet and busied himself behind the bar. He washed the empty pewter mugs and small rum glasses in cold, greasy water, remembering the innkeeper's rule: all dregs went into three jars beneath the bar. They were marked clearly: 'RUM', 'PORTER' and 'ALE'. Old Feltham enjoyed a nip now and then – 'to keep the heat in and cold out...'

So busy was Mungo for the rest of the day, he had no time to think about the mysterious sketch. Slops, sweeping, serving, skivvying came first and last. It wasn't until he was back in the stable that he had time for private thoughts.

He gazed sadly at the straw hollow made by the black boy's body. Something made him kneel down and tenderly touch the wispy straw. He smelt the lingering dampness of the boy's sodden shirt and breeches. Sorrowfully he recalled the lined face, the grateful half-smile, Mungo's sea-going plans for them both – and then the boy's ice-cold fingers.

Mungo's expression changed as he recalled the livid scar on the boy's chest; it must have been done with a red-hot branding iron! *Cripes!* It hurt just to think of it.

Mungo patted his skinny midriff to reassure himself of the paper's safety. The stiff parchment now lay against his own skin; it seemed to connect both of them in some flesh-and-blood bond. Carefully, he eased the paper out and laid it reverently in the straw hollow – like a posy of flowers upon a grave.

'And I don't even know your name,' he murmured, as if the boy were lying there listening. 'You *must* have a name. Everyone has a name. I can't think of you without a name. Wait, I'll find one for you.'

He screwed up his eyes and thought hard. Adam (his father's name)? Jonah? Bert? Rob? None seemed to fit the ill-fated boy.

His eyes dwelt on the rough sketch of the clipper and the words scrawled underneath: *ABENA*. Could that be his name?

'I know,' he exclaimed. 'You can be Aba. That'll do, eh, Aba?'

A snort from Bessie reminded him it was way past bedtime. As he nestled in the straw blanketed with potato sacks, his mind wouldn't let him rest. Somehow he had to unlock the mystery. He owed it to his dead pal. It was now *his* duty to discover the paper's secret. But he couldn't do it alone. He needed someone to explain the clipper and matchstick figures, the word ABENA. Who did he know? Who could he trust to help him? He needed someone who knew foreign parts.

His dad might have helped. He'd crossed the Atlantic, he'd told stories of the Spanish Main, of raiding Spanish ships laden down with gold treasure in the Caribbean, of mysterious islands in the sun –

Jamaica, Hispaniola, Barbados. But Dad's bones were lying on the seabed.

Wait a minute... There was someone. Someone who knew foreign parts and foreign words. Someone who was foreign himself – the old salt who'd talked about pirates and heroes that night. The man had been darker of skin and beard than most of the regulars. And he spoke in a low sing-song voice with lots of 'ees' and 'aahs' – *'ees good, aah?'*

Perhaps he could help Mungo unlock the secret of the matchstick ship.

Thirteen

The next evening, Mungo kept one eye on the inn door
as he went about his chores. Sure enough, round about
eight, a short, slim figure slipped in and took his seat in
one corner.

As the evening wore on and the chatter rose up with
the spiralling smoke, so the man's voice sank down to
his boots. It was as if the notes had to battle up from
the depths of some dark cavern.

When the man was quite alone, puffing quietly on a
white clay pipe, Mungo moved across to clear away the
empties.

'Excuse me, sir,' he began politely. 'May I take your
glass?'

The man grunted between puffs, rather like Bessie
the mare. His thoughts were evidently far away, his eyes
staring dully into the distance, as if he were dreaming
of his homeland.

Mungo tried again. 'Sir, may I ask a favour?'

That brought the man back to port. He peered at
the boy through the fug, as if he were a stray cat
brushing against his leg.

'*Si*, ask,' was all he said. He removed the pipe from
his mouth, knocked out the coarse black grains on

the heel of his boot and refilled the bowl.

Mungo fished the scrap of paper from his shirt and laid it on a dry edge of the table. He dropped no hint about the paper's source – just said he'd swept it up with the sawdust, old rind and spittle.

With a shrug, the man bent forward, the stiff tail of his beard moving back and forth, up and down, as if tracing each line of the two sketches. Finally, his black eyes rose slowly to meet the boy's.

Mungo held his gaze and saw pity in his face.

'Mmmm, ee's sad, ah?'

'What does it mean?' Mungo asked impatiently.

In the long silence that followed, he noticed that the man's beard jutted out stubbornly below lips pressed together as tightly as a clam. Clearly he knew more than he was prepared to tell. If Mungo was to winkle the story out of him, he'd have to gain his confidence.

He decided on a change of tack.

'What does the word under the ship mean?'

The Spaniard read it three times, each time changing the accent: 'Ah-been-ah. A-been-a, Abeen-ah.' He shook his head.

'Ee's no English, no Spanish. Could be African.'

Africa again!

Mungo told him about the black boy, how he'd come upon him by the scaffold, taken him home and looked after him. He described the letters 'SV' branded on his chest.

'*Si,* eet fits. Thees ship ees slaver. She take slaves from Africa to Caribbean, maybe Jamaica.'

Mungo looked puzzled. He'd heard his father mention Jamaica a few times – something to do with spices and rum. But he didn't know where it was.

'Where's Jamaica?'

'Jamaica? Christopher Columbus discovered eet in 1494. Spanish till England stole eet, about eighty years ago, in 1655.'

Just then a shout rang out: 'Mungo!'

'Coming.'

Snatching up the paper, he skipped off to finish his chores.

By the time he returned to the shadowy corner, the man had gone. So that was that. But as he went to lift the empty glass, he noticed a scrap of paper underneath. On it was scrawled a brief message:

'Jetty. Ten. Tomorrow.'

Mungo glanced round to see if anyone was watching. Evidently no one was.

He did not notice the weasel-like man with the black eye-patch sitting on the other side of the partition. If he had, he would have seen the man's lips curl in a cruel grin. He had overheard everything.

Mungo busied himself until midnight. Then he hurried home, to dream of waving palms and sandy shores.

Fourteen

When Abena stepped out on to the deck, she felt a strange sensation. The ground beneath her feet was shifting, as if she'd mistaken a log for a crocodile. It took her several minutes to get her sea legs, as she learned to sway from side to side to the ship's rocking. She heard odd sounds all about her: screaming seagulls and water lapping against creaking timbers, for all the world like chattering monkeys. Then she almost jumped out of her skin as, above her head, thunder bellowed from the wind in the sails like a giant bird flapping its vast wings.

The sounds of the sea were bad enough, but she was horrified to hear human groans and screams coming from beneath her feet. In the middle of the deck was a gated hatchway from which terrifying noises were drifting up, along with a stench even more vile and overpowering than that inside the *barracoon*.

She was soon to discover that as many as six hundred bodies were already packed on shelves at the bottom of the ship. They were chained to each other by the neck and ankle, and stowed so tightly they had to lie between each other's legs, spoon fashion, with no possibility of changing position by night or day.

There was less room than a man would have in his coffin.

The slaves had been there for a whole month, wallowing in their own vomit, urine and faeces, stifling in the suffocating heat, blinded by darkness; scores had already died of disease, lack of air, even the will to live. Each morning, sailors dragged out the dead and tossed them overboard with the bilge.

Now at last the ship's cargo was complete: the final batch of a hundred slaves had arrived to fill the last nook and cranny of the slaver.

Captain Bibby, master of the *Sea Venture*, was a 'tight packing' man. Unlike the 'loose packers', who provided slaves with more room and food to reduce deaths on the second stage of the three-cornered voyage, Captain Bibby was prepared to lose fifty to sixty slaves on a larger cargo for a higher return. If the survivors turned out to be walking skeletons, they could be fattened up in a Caribbean slave yard before auction. Most Guinean captains followed Bibby's example. After all, a black man was worth exactly what his flesh would bring at market. If his flesh brought nothing, he could be disposed of like a horse with a broken leg.

As Abena was to discover, she and the other forty girls and women were to be spared the fate of the men down in the dingy, stifling, stinking hold. During the daytime they were able to wander about the ship;

at night they were chained to the bare boards below the quarterdeck, between the weapon stores and the officers' quarters.

With dusk falling, the women were served their first warm meal for several weeks. Two brawny sailors carried in a large pot of stewed yams and dumped it in the middle of the floor between decks. Judging from the greasy fat floating on top, it had been cooked with a few lumps of salt beef taken from the crew's rations. Along with this food, the women each received half a pint of water in a pannikin.

Like the rest, Abena had no bowl or spoon, so she had to dip her fingers into the pot to eat. Since everyone was starving, those strongest and closest to the pot got the lion's share. With her mother ill and Kwame taken with the men, Abena and Afi were no match for the bigger women. This was a case of survival of the fittest.

Fortunately for Abena and other young girls, many of the initial gobblers were having difficulty keeping the stew down; so they had to abandon the pot for the slop buckets, while the youngest and weakest scooped the remaining food into their cupped hands, licking their fingers hungrily. As soon as the pot was clean and the metal cup of water had been passed round, the women were shackled together for the night.

It was a calm evening as the *Sea Venture* set sail for Jamaica. With a fair wind at their backs they made good headway through the Gulf of Guinea, bearing westward along the equator into that dangerous part men called 'the Sea of Thunder'. As evening wore on, the wind fell away and, at around midnight, a dead calm and prickly heat descended. A little later came an eerie sound, and high overhead the air began to echo to a faint, hollow booming. Then, without warning, the storm broke.

The waves rose in mounting fury, each overtopping the other until soon the sea was like a roaring, ravenous monster. As the ship pitched helplessly in the tossing waves, it was driven back towards the shore. The sailors could see white-crested waves beating madly on the inshore rocks and rushing up the shelving cliffs.

What with the bucking and lack of air – for the hatchway had been covered with tarpaulin – many women fainted between decks from the foul air and heat. Their wailing fell on deaf ears, for all hands were on deck battling against the storm. At some distance both sea and land could be seen vividly in the glare of lightning.

Meanwhile, banks of cloud came drifting over the ocean, so dank and cold you'd think the souls of those lost at sea were reaching out clammy hands to the living. Now and again the cloud cleared, and for some distance both sea and land could be seen vividly in the glare of lightning. A sheltering bay beckoned – if only they could reach it.

All at once, a blinding flash lit up another ship with all sails set. It was leaping from wave to wave as it rushed headlong towards the beach. Then, with a shuddering crash and groaning of timbers, it pitched on to the shore, its mast toppling into the sea, to be quickly swept away on the tide.

The crew of the *Sea Venture* watched the vessel's plight helplessly, praying they too would not share its fate.

Captain Bibby, shocked by the ship's fate, was determined to ride out the storm. He couldn't risk a run for the bay past those jagged rocks. Although they passed a storm-tossed night, by dawn the worst of the gale had passed, the blinding rain had eased to a shower, and they were able to steer into the bay and drop anchor.

Eager to explore the stranded brig, the Captain set off for shore in the long-boat with a few sailors. The ship was lying on her side, rocked gently by the foaming waves. But such was the force with which it had pitched on to land that most of the hull was now high and dry halfway up the sand.

Captain Bibby was the first to climb aboard, stepping over the lower starboard rail and hauling himself up the sloping, rocking deck. As his head came level with the helm, he stifled a cry of horror. For there before him, lashed to the helm, was a corpse, mouth gaping, head drooping, body swinging to and fro with every motion of the ship.

The man was fastened by his hands, tied one over the other to the spokes of the wheel by a rosary: the crucifix was clenched tightly in the palm of one hand, while the set of beads was wound round the wrists and wheel; it had cut through to the bone. Such was the look of terror on the dead man's face that all who saw it knew it would haunt them for the rest of their lives.

Bibby's party found nothing else on board. The ship was a Spanish cargo vessel; she had been stripped bare, presumably by the same heartless brigands who had served the Captain so cruelly.

'Only one man could treat his victims so badly,' Captain Bibby muttered. 'This bears all the signs of Blackbeard, the worst pirate alive!'

Fifteen

Back on his own ship, the Captain had to sit tight, waiting for a breeze and the outgoing tide. He was not in the best of tempers. Any delay risked the ship running short of provisions before they reached port. With a fair wind in the sails, Bibby reckoned on a three-to-four week crossing. But if the ship was becalmed in the doldrums or driven back by storms, it might take more than three months – and everyone would be on short rations. The ship was victualled for only eight weeks. Either he'd have to starve the slaves, or chuck a few overboard.

He need not have worried. As the sun rose next morning, the skies had cleared and a fiery heat greeted the day. On shore the tallest palms began to bend and sway gracefully, steadily picking up speed until they gyrated to a swishing chorus of palm music. A breeze swept across the land to dance unobstructed over the water. It ruffled the surface of the sea, plucking up tipsy plumes of foam that tripped and frolicked across the swell, rocking the ship and flapping its canvas sails.

'Ready, aye, ready!' bellowed the Captain, as men scurried about the deck and clambered up the rigging. Each knew his post as the *Sea Venture* ploughed through the waves and fairly flew out to sea, leaving Africa behind.

'All clear?' Bibby bawled up to the look-out.

'Aye-aye, sir. Horizon clear.'

Bibby was uneasy. Like many old sea dogs he was superstitious and hated having women on board. Not so his officers. In the middle of the night, Abena had woken up to a commotion coming from the far end of the deck. She could hear a woman shouting and crying, 'No, no, no!' In the dim light she could see a man in uniform dragging the poor girl away to a cabin. She wanted to cry, 'Stop!' But a hand on her wrist from the woman beside her stilled the cry in her throat.

'Hush! Hush!' came a low, hoarse voice. 'There's nothing we can do.'

Abena was so angry, she hissed, 'Don't you care?'

For a moment, the woman was silent. Then, with a sob in her voice, she said,

'If I could, I'd gladly offer myself in exchange. That poor girl was torn away from her husband and child, branded on her breast and thrown into the bilge at the bottom of a dug-out canoe. Now this! Prey to a drunken officer!'

Abena was horrified. What if the same fate awaited her or her sister? She felt sorry for her first hasty words to the woman.

'Is she from your village?' she asked.

'She's my daughter.'

Less than an hour later the young woman returned, moaning softly and sobbing herself to sleep. No one said a word.

Next morning, the same two sailors brought in the first meal of the day, a pot of boiled cornmeal. This time, the older woman next to Abena took charge, rationing out the food so that everyone received a handful of the cold cereal. All the women treated her with respect, as if she was an *obeah* or medicine woman.

After breakfast, the women were allowed up on deck. Abena looked around her in amazement: water, water, endless rolling blue water, with not a palm tree in sight. Above her head, vast grey cloths billowed out on lofty poles and ropes, filled with wind.

For the first time, she had a good look at the crew. In full daylight they seemed paler than a crocodile's underbelly and uglier than a baboon's backside. Their heads and faces were covered in strange long hair of various colours: yellow and red, black and brown, white and grey. Never had she seen an army of meaner-looking bandits, all bearing the scars of war: some missing an eye, an ear or a leg or arm, some with backs pitted with knife cuts or the whip's lash, many with rotting teeth or no teeth at all.

Their resemblance to apes was reinforced by the ease with which they swung from pole to pole, yanking on the ropes as if flying through the forest on lianas, hooting and barking at each other.

Her wonderment was ended by a whip descending on the women's backs, forcing them into a huddle about the main mast. When they were rounded up, like goats in a pen, two sailors approached with a large tub. This time it was not food, but sea-water.

Cursing loudly, the two men began dousing the women and scrubbing them down with long-handled brushes. Since none of the women wore more than a shame-cloth round their waists, the salt water stung like live coals on the women's still-livid scars and festering sores. Abena couldn't help herself. She cried out in pain as the water frothed pink and scarlet at her feet.

Their ablutions over, the women were shoved back towards the mast. They then had to watch as batches of men were brought up from below to undergo the same process. It was soon obvious that the men were in a far worse state than the women. Many had been entombed in the hold so long, they couldn't even open their eyes. All were covered in filth that must have stunk five miles downwind; the storm had caused the skin on some elbows to wear away to the bare bone. They too had to run the gauntlet of drenching sea-water and stiff bristles, their screams mingling with the curses of the sailors.

In the third batch of slaves, Abena was both glad and sorry to see Kwame. He was covering his eyes with his free hand as he shuffled along, chained by the ankle to a taller, older man, trying to breathe, opening and closing his cracked lips to take hungry gulps of fresh air.

Abena gasped as her brother suddenly stumbled, fell headlong and vomited over the deck. She seemed to feel the lash herself as it bit into his flesh, bringing him quickly to his feet. Seeing his mother and sisters, however, he smiled awkwardly, ashamed of betraying any weakness.

After cleaning some two hundred and fifty men, the Master-at-Arms stepped forward, brandishing a pistol above his head. It was the signal for a bizarre ritual to commence.

Sixteen

One of the sailors was holding what looked like a pig's bladder stuck with pipes; this he began blowing and squeezing to produce a wailing noise, like women grieving at a funeral. A second man then banged an upturned kettle with a stick, while a black man thumped a broken African drum. While the slaves looked on in bewilderment, the Master-at-Arms bawled out something that sounded like 'Joomp!', then started to leap up and down like a demented chimpanzee.

'I think he wants us to jump in the air,' said the *obeah*, standing with her arm round her daughter's shoulders.

She showed the way, advancing to the gap between women and men and jumping up and down in short hops to the drumbeats and the wheezing pig's bladder. She gestured to the men to do the same; but many had such swollen and bleeding feet that they just stood staring, thinking she'd gone mad. Only when the sailors began laying about them with whips did some slaves make an effort, clanking their chains and pretending to jump.

To the obvious delight of the sailors, the *obeah*

danced about the deck, goading the shackled men to join her in the 'dance of Africa', and calling on the women, 'Jump! Jump! All of you, jump!' Not understanding, they nonetheless hopped up and down and swayed to and fro, caught up in the drumbeat rhythm.

The sailors beamed and cheered, clapping their hands at the success of this exercise hour.

Bounding over to the half-hearted menfolk, the woman leading the dance this time cried out in Akan, 'Dance, dance! Sing, sing! We shall survive! Death to the slavers!'

As her meaning sank home, first one, then another pair of shackled men shuffled from side to side, until everyone was dancing and taking up the song:

'We shall survive! Death to the slavers!'

'We shall survive! Death to the slavers!'

It was the song of the women that rang out loudest, soaring up and over the ship, up and over the waves. And it brought comfort to the slaves, who imagined they were dancing and singing back home in their villages. To the grinning crew, listening to the chants and watching the half-naked men and women dancing was right royal entertainment. Several joined in the chants, trying to mimic the words, 'Death to the slavers!'

Amid all the excitement, no one seemed to notice a young woman sidling towards the ship's rail. It was the *obeah*'s daughter. With a set, determined face as if in a trance, she was now standing beside the gunwale. Too late, a guard went to grab her; but she slipped from his grasp, scrambled over the rail and dived into the sea.

In the hubbub that ensued, from the poop deck the Captain let fly a string of curses at the crew and orders to the nearest sailors.

Even if anyone had been foolish enough to attempt a rescue, yells from the rigging soon deterred them. As all eyes followed the pointing fingers, slaves and seamen were horrified to see grey fins ploughing swiftly through the waves straight towards the floundering girl. A blood-curdling shriek pierced the air as she vanished beneath the waves, leaving a red trail behind her.

No one danced or sang any more. No more curses fell. No one tried to stop the *obeah* as she made her way below, her face expressionless, to be alone with her grief.

Seventeen

After finishing his early morning duties, Mungo took a break. With Mr Feltham gone to market in the Camber, he had an hour's rest. So he scuttled off, unnoticed, just before ten. The jetty was no more than a stone's throw from the inn.

It was a bright day with orange sunbeams dancing on the waves. Mungo loved the moods of the sea. No colour, no shade, no wave was ever the same; each was special, caught in the fleeting moment, never to return. Today it was calm and content, smiling broadly.

So was the boy's waiting friend. He was sitting on the jetty, legs dangling over the edge just above the lapping waves. When he saw Mungo he gave a cheery wave, calling out, 'Mungee, over here.'

Mungo squatted down beside him. The man smelt pleasantly of cloves and tobacco.

'I don't have long,' Mungo said. 'Must get back before I'm missed.'

'*Si*, I understand,' the man said with a slight frown.

As if at a signal, they both looked round – to ensure there were no eavesdroppers. The coast was clear.

The Spaniard focused his eyes on the breakers beyond the harbour mouth. Then he rocked to and fro, before beginning.

He talked of the Conquistadors who first sailed the Spanish Main, seized land from the native people and took their treasure – gold and silver – shipping it back to Spain. They settled in the New World, making the natives their slaves. But soon the English snatched the Caribbean islands from them, developing sugar and tobacco plantations there.

First the English used the natives as labour, but they died like flies or ran away. That is when the slave trade started. The English transported thousands of Africans to toil on the plantations. But not only Africans. The British deported thousands of Scottish and Irish prisoners, as well as other 'undesirables' to work in their colonies; they were treated as badly as the African slaves.

Suddenly Mungo realised.

'Oh, I see now. The clipper is a slaver. The matchstick figures are slaves!'

'*Si, si,* ees right. Your black boy, he slave. The Master, he brand 'ees mark on boy: SV – the ship's initials, ah?'

'But how did the boy end up with pirates?'

The Spaniard shrugged.

'Captured? Escaped, no?'

He jabbed a finger at the second matchstick sketch.

'Ees dangerous.'

Mungo didn't understand.

'Ees law on numbers of slaves in ship hold. Here...'

It was clear from the figures stacked top to toe, lying cheek by jowl, that they were packed together like apples in a barrel. Mungo didn't need anyone to tell him how important the sketch could be, in the right hands. He knew there were people – Abolitionists – campaigning against slavery.

Mungo was caught between a desire to learn more and his fear of Mr Feltham boxing his ears for being late.

'I must go,' he cried suddenly, 'or Mr Feltham'll have my guts for garters. Thank you, sir, thank you for telling me all this.'

The Spaniard smiled sadly, putting a finger to his lips.

'Let eet be secret,' he said. 'Eef slave-catchers are about and they no know ee's dead, or eef they learn of sketch...' He made the sign of a dirk slitting his throat.

'Oh, yes,' Mungo said, getting to his feet.

He stared the Spaniard in the eye and said firmly, 'They won't get the secret out of me!'

Don Jose shook his head.

'See you later,' Mungo called, as he scuttled off.

Eighteen

When Mungo burrowed under the straw and sacks that night, the Spaniard's tale would not let him go. He was whisked off to Africa. Josh's snores became the low rumblings of slave-hunters, stalking their prey. Bessie's whinnies were the screams of captured girls and boys. The wind and crash of the waves outside were ships transporting slaves to Jamaica. Even the rats had a part: they became the plantation owners and merchants, branding each slave with their initials – *hiss-ss, sizz-zzle*.

All at once, Mungo heard another sound, one that had no place in the slave tale. Someone – or something – was prowling about outside! Every so often Mungo caught a footfall on the cobblestones; then came a hissing curse as the prowler banged his shins against the water-butt. Flickering shadows bounced off the rafters and inside walls from a lantern. Who on earth could it be?

It was well past midnight. He'd never had intruders before. Tramps wouldn't be carrying a lantern or combing the street at that time of night. Of course, it could be the press gang on the prowl. Or were they horse thieves? Bessie and Josh seemed to think so: they were suddenly awake, whinnying softly and snorting at the unexpected sounds and flickering light.

Horse thieves was the most likely explanation. If so, Mungo was in deep trouble. He couldn't do much against men armed with clubs, dirks or pistols. But he'd do his best! He'd fight tooth and nail. No one would steal the drays without a fight!

He caught his breath. Someone was fumbling at the stable door… For the first time, Mungo wished he'd slotted home the heavy wooden bar. He'd never bothered before. There was nothing to stop thieves breaking in, slitting his throat and stealing the drays.

What was he to do? He had no weapon to defend himself with.

He decided to bury himself in the straw, then attack the thieves as they led out the drays. That way he might delay them, giving the animals a chance to escape.

By the time the doors creaked open, Mungo was nowhere to be seen.

Since he slept in what he stood up in, coat and scarf and all, he had left no tell-tale signs. No shirts draped neatly over a chair! His chief worry was that the straw tickling his ears and nose might make him sneeze.

He could make out two voices, hoarse and low. As the pair got used to the dim light, the voices grew louder and bolder.

'Where the 'ell is the kid?'

'Ee's gotta be 'ere somewhere.'

Mungo trembled beneath the chaff.

Could it be him they were after? But why?

All he could think of was the scrap of paper.

The horses were now kicking up a rumpus, champing and pawing the floor.

Suddenly, above the neighing, he heard a thrashing noise: the men were tramping through the straw. Sooner or later, they were bound to find him. It was just a matter of time...

One of the men gave a yelp.

'Wassat? Oh my gawd, it's a bleedin' great rat!'

As the lantern swung about, the other man howled, 'The place's infested with 'em. I don't want one of them blighters biting off me toes.'

'Here, Blood,' came the higher voice, 'pass us the light. I'll see if he's in the stalls with them nags.'

A moment later, amid rumbling protests from the drays, the man growled, 'Nah, he ain't here. He must've got wind of us coming. Now, how we gonna get our slave bounty?'

'We'll nab his mate at the inn and slit his gizzard if 'e don't tell us where 'e's 'iding. Come on, Weasel, let's shift our bones out of here and get some shut-eye.'

Mungo lay as still as a log, barely daring to breathe.

So the prowlers weren't after horses. Don Jose was right: the black slave was what they were after. They obviously didn't know he was dead and chucked into the briny.

When Mungo thought the coast was clear, he thrust an arm through the straw and hauled himself up.

What now? If he went to the inn, they'd be waiting for him. If he remained at the stable, they'd come for him anyway. Where was he to go? He had no relatives or friends, no one he could confide in – apart from Don Jose. And he'd only spoken to him twice…

Who were the two villains? *'Blood'* and *'Weasel'*, they'd called each other. That meant nothing to him. Rough types they sounded, from their voices. He fancied he recognised the hoarse, rum-soaked tones of the one called Weasel. Maybe he'd served him at the inn.

What was he to do? He couldn't just up and go. The poor horses needed feeding every day. He'd have to tell the owner, Mr Jeffs.

This gave him an idea. Mr Jeffs had helped him once. He was a kindly man who'd told Mungo how sorry he was to take the money his father owed him. 'A debt's a debt,' he'd said regretfully. But now and then he'd call at the inn with a little something for Mungo: some plum jam, seed cake, meat pie – 'to keep the wolf from the door,' he'd say. And he'd let Mungo sleep in the stable.

What if Mungo sought his help to escape – out of reach of those cut-throats? A passage on a ship, perhaps. It was his only hope.

He'd go and see Mr Jeffs first thing in the morning.

Nineteen

The rest of the night passed in fitful sleep, with Mungo jumping at the slightest sound.

He drifted in and out of sleep. In his dreams, he was surrounded by cutthroats, reaching for his neck and battling with the rats ringed about him.

He was thankful when the dim light of dawn began to filter through the grimy windows. Daylight was less scary than the dark.

Quickly he fed and watered the horses. Then he peered out of the window and poked his head round the stable doors. No one about. Judging by the sun, it was just after seven, too early to wake Mr Jeffs. He had an hour or so to kill.

Pulling his worldly possessions – the ragged coat and grey muffler – tightly about him, he slipped outside and hurried along the seashore, scattering the seagulls on the shingle. It was icy cold and misty over the sea. He could barely make out Gosport on the far side of the harbour mouth. Making a detour round the Camber's fishing smacks, he regained the shoreline by the Round Tower. Once on Sallyport beach, he scuffed over shells and pebbles, stamping crossly on the purple-green seaweed.

'Why did I have to befriend that black urchin?' he muttered. 'Too soppy, that's me. Now look at the mess I'm in. Up to my neck in it. All because of him. Him! Him! Him!' Each popping seaweed emphasised the 'Him'.

But Mungo's anger soon passed. He knew he'd do the same again.

'Poor little bleeder, it wasn't his fault I took the paper from his shirt. He was as dead as a doornail by then, anyhow. Poor Aba, God rest his soul.'

As he reached the water's edge, he looked out over the waves, staring sightlessly at the incoming tide.

All at once, he switched his gaze from the tidal clash to something closer to shore. At first glance, it resembled a clump of seaweed floating on the tide. It bobbed up and down in the lapping waves amid a debris of white-bellied crab-shells, cuttlefish, frayed rope and two dark-green bottles. The seaweedy nest was caught on bulky flotsam. A sodden log... fish carcass... boat wreckage...? Hard to tell. With a troubled sigh, Mungo raised his gaze to the horizon. The early mist was lifting and the sky was now a dove-grey canopy shading into the sea.

The morning was lit by pale sunshine. Melting slivers of ice still encrusted the sea cabbages and cucumbers dotted along the beach, and at the margin of the sea the cleansing tide was driving out the shoreline scum. So blinding was the sun that Mungo had to shield his eyes from the glare reflected off the sea.

Lost in thought, he was caught unawares by a sudden surge of tide that swamped his feet. He hopped back, glancing testily at the hissing foam. It had deposited a heap of flotsam on his wet feet.

'Right, matey, I'll teach you,' he growled. Bending down for a handful of pebbles to hurl at the receding waves, he leaned forward, took aim at the tangled seaweed and let fly.

'Gotcha!' He shouted vengefully, as the pebble struck the clump with a squelchy thud. 'That's for soaking my feet! Serves you...'

The cry caught in his throat. There was something odd about the floating mass the tide was bringing in. He half expected a green-bearded sea god to rise up, shaking a three-pronged fork and roaring, 'Who hit me on the head?'

But what he saw was far more sinister than raging Neptune.

First he made out a dark, bearded face below straggly green hair. Then he saw a jagged crimson gash curving from ear to ear beneath the jutting beard. At the other end, the shiny toes of two boots were bobbing up and down like floats on a fishing line.

With a shock he recognised the body. It was Don Jose.

Twenty

If the ship's Captain was heartless towards the slaves, he was scarcely more human to his own men. To him, sailors were mere items in the ledger; what is more, they were of less value than slaves. When he needed replacements, all he had to do was click his fingers to the press gang in Liverpool or Bristol, and they would bring him 'volunteers'. In any port of call – whether Jamaica, Barbados or Charlestown – he could round up drunks and down-and-outs desperate for money to spend on more drink.

Like slaves, his own kind needed to be starved and flogged regularly, he believed, to make them toe the line.

Shortly after the loss of the young black girl, Captain Bibby ordered all hands on deck. Along with the women and last batch of male slaves, they were to witness the usual Guinea Captain's punishment for dereliction of duty. Someone had to pay for letting the girl escape and disobeying his order to dive in after her. Standing on the poop deck, brandishing the Bible, he declared to all and sundry: 'An eye for an eye, a tooth for a tooth.'

It didn't matter to him whether it was a black or

a blue eye, a black or a white tooth.

Abena watched as a narrow wooden plank was lashed firmly to the gunwale so that three quarters of it overlapped the rail above the open sea. Two seamen, dressed smartly in bell-bottomed, navy-blue trousers, white calico shirts and broad-brimmed black shiny hats, stood either side of the plank. Slung round the shoulders of each was a drum. At an order from the Captain, they raised their drumsticks and beat a slow, monotonous *rat-tat-tat, rat-tat-tat*.

As the drum roll grew in volume, a wretched bare-footed sailor in crumpled, striped jersey and canvas pantaloons was dragged forward, clanking his ankle irons over the deck. He was a skinny runt of a man, with a black patch over one eye and straggly ginger hair. As a deck hand removed his chains, for a brief moment his one eye gleamed hopefully. But a look at the plank told him his fate.

Under the Captain's stern gaze, two burly men seized his arms and legs. While one blindfolded him, the other lifted him up bodily until his feet were planted on the plank. Kicking and screaming, he tried several times to scramble back to the deck. But the two men pushed him forward.

The poor man fell to his knees, clasping the sides of the plank, crying and begging to be spared. But a cutlass point forced him closer and closer to the far end. Finally, he lost his balance, toppled over and hit the water with a splash.

Abena couldn't look. A shoal of sharks was following the clipper across the ocean, somehow knowing that they were going to enjoy regular feeds.

To a final roll on the drums, the Captain dismissed his crew.

The batch of male slaves was detained on deck, free to take clean air into their burning lungs, but not permitted to move from the spot. Unlike the women, they were barred from setting foot on the rest of the ship. The reason for this soon became clear.

A beefy, red-faced sailor inspecting women huddled by the main mast suddenly pulled out Afi and Abena. At first, Abena thought with dread that they were to share the fate of the *obeah*'s daughter. But no: the sailor roughly thrust into their hands two odd wooden poles.

Were they to scrub the deck where the skinny sailor had messed himself before walking the plank? Evidently not, for the Red Face was gesturing them to follow him down below, down to the very bottom of the ship where the male slaves were kept.

Never in all her twelve years, even in the foul *barracoon*, had Abena experienced anything like it. The moment they stepped down into the hold, the stench hit the sisters full in the face in a thick blast of poisonous vapour. As they tried to block it out, they stared all about them in horror: the wooden shelves were covered in a thick grey paste of filth.

So nauseating was the heat, stench and foul air that they were both immediately overcome. Abi pitched forward on to the floor in a faint while Abena dropped to her knees, vomiting. Surely no human being could survive in this cess pit?

The sailor accompanying them must have been hardened to the stink, though he'd taken the precaution of removing his clothes and gagging himself with a wet cloth. He had no pity for the girls: using one of the poles he laid about Afi mercilessly, shrieking at her, *'Oop! Oop! Oop!'* With Abena's help she rapidly came round and was hauled to her feet, retching. The naked sailor now made jerky movements with his arms as if he were rowing a canoe. In the dim light filtering through the bars of the open hatchway, it seemed to the girls that the fumes had driven him mad.

As he grabbed the wooden poles, it suddenly dawned on them: he was going through the motions of cleaning!

The horrified sisters realised that he expected them to scrape the filth off the shelves with the long-handled hoe, sweep the mess on to the floor with a stiff-headed broom and shovel it into a large bucket. When the bucket was full, the sailor himself was evidently going to drag it back along the gangway, bump it up the steps and empty it into the sea.

A few blows across their shoulders with the hoe forced the girls into action. While Afi scraped and swept, Abena shovelled up the stinking mess of vomit and mucous, urine and faeces, blood and bile; into the bucket it went with a splash. In the dingy half-light, the sisters slowly worked their way, inch by inch, along the gangway. Behind them came one of the overseers, carrying two pails of sour-smelling vinegar heated up with red-hot bullets; this he used to flush the scrubbed shelves and floor, driving out the foul air. The vinegar fumes made the girls' eyes water, but that was preferable to what went before. Abena quickly learned to take short breaths through clenched teeth and, now and then, pressed her nose into her naked armpit, glad for once of her own sweaty smell.

Once the forward section of the hold was scrubbed and swabbed to the overseer's satisfaction, he shouted up for the slaves to be brought back down to their quarters. That was the signal for the middle section slaves to take their turn aloft.

The revolting work started all over again: scraping, sweeping, shovelling, emptying, flushing and swabbing. Afi and Abena swapped jobs, with the younger girl now scraping the shelf boards. As her head came level with one of the shelves, she suddenly felt something thick and furry brush her cheek; before she could react, a cold, whiskery nose sniffed at her tightly-clamped mouth. It was a large rat! Trembling in fear, and with her hands occupied, Abena abruptly snapped her teeth together, sending the rat scuttling away. In relief, she let out a cry: *'Ai-yee-ee-ee!'*

Out of the darkness she caught a low whisper in her own tongue. It made her jump. Apart from the women, no one had spoken to her since she'd come on board.

'Don't worry about the rats. They won't bite unless you're dead. Then it won't matter anyway.'

The voice was calm and reassuring, evidently that of a young man. Dimly she made out a tall figure lying on a shelf, where the ship was widest. Presumably they stacked the tall ones amidships and the short ones in the bows and stern.

'Who are you? Where are you from?' she whispered.

'My name is Teiko,' came back the low voice. 'I'm from Kumasi. And you?'

Looking behind her to make sure the overseer was out of earshot, Abena told her story. As she was speaking, she could hear an eerie howling coming from the stern; it sounded rather like a cow in labour, but was more a moan of melancholy anguish than of physical pain.

'What's that terrible noise?' she asked.

'Oh that! We get so used to noises down here: men dying, men in pain, tribal enemies shackled together. But that howl is special. It's the cry of a man dreaming of home, of the wife and mother he left behind, of his village. When he wakes up, he finds himself in the hold of a slave ship, far from home, being taken God knows where.'

'How can you stand it down here?'

For a moment the man was silent, wondering how to explain. Then he muttered, 'Some don't. They believe they return home when they die. So they starve themselves to death; after a while, they fall into a trance and slowly fade away.'

'This hell-hole is enough to drive anyone mad,' Abena murmured.

'You're right. But madness doesn't save them. Do you know what the Red Faces do? They flog them to death – just in case they're putting it on. Some are simply clubbed on the head and tossed overboard.'

'What do they do to the wailers?'

'The chief has his own method of curing them. He cuts off their heads if they refuse food. That's to show that if we're set on going home, we'll have to go without our heads.'

Abena began to realise how fortunate the women were up aloft. Life on board was bearable for most of them: daylight, fresh air and freedom to exercise. By contrast, the men wallowed in their own filth, in darkness, shackled together, with no space even to turn over. No wonder some gave in to despair.

She made up her mind.

'We women must do all we can to keep your spirits up,' she hissed, 'just as the *obeah* did this morning with her warrior dance.'

'You're right, Abena,' he said. 'Men may be stronger

in arm, but African women are stronger in spirit. If the Red Faces understood that, they wouldn't give you so much freedom. We must find a way of fighting back. But we have to bide our time and pick our moment carefully. Our enemy is powerful, he has guns and swords.'

'Perhaps we can take weapons for ourselves,' she said.

He thought carefully about that, for he was silent for a time. At last he said, 'Tell your women to keep their eyes and ears open. You can wander almost where you like, all over the boat, apart from the hold. Only women cleaners are allowed down here. You and your sister can be go-betweens, keeping us informed and taking messages.'

'What do you want us to do?' she asked.

'Find out where the guns are kept and who has keys to the weapon stores. If you can somehow steal keys to unlock our chains and open the armoury, we can grab the guns, and turn the tables on the Red Faces.'

As they were speaking, the tub-trundler could be heard clumping down the steps with an empty bucket, ready for the sisters to fill up again.

'We'll do our best,' whispered Abena.

She could tell from the overseer's angry curses that he'd heard her talking to someone. His raised fist thrust in her face warned her that no talking was permitted in the hold. Dutifully, she bent her head and shovelled as fast as she could.

When she and Afi returned on deck, they both hungrily gulped down the clean, salty air. Although they were able to purge their lungs, the cloying stench of the hold remained on them; that was obvious from the way the crew steered clear; some of their own women wrinkled their noses and turned away. Even after washing and scrubbing their skins in a bucket of sea-water, the stink lingered on their hair and loin-cloths for days afterwards. And just when it was fading, they were forced to go through the twice-weekly ordeal all over again.

The one advantage of their job as cleaners was being able to communicate with the men. Abena told the other women of her conversation and the plan to gather information. Not all the women spoke the Akan language; nonetheless, it was soon made plain by eyes and hands what was needed of them.

In the hard days ahead, their dream of taking over the ship and making the crew work for them gave the slaves hope.

Twenty-one

Each morning, led by the *obeah,* the women danced and sang to lift the men's spirits. The *obeah* would begin swaying sinuously on the spot. She moved gracefully to and fro, undulating from the hips as every part of her body responded to the drum-beat. Her long lissom arms curled upwards menacingly, like a cobra about to strike, then wove graceful circles in the air, like a sycamore seed twirling lightly to the ground.

Behind her, the girls and women copied her every movement, as if born to a rhythm and grace that belonged to eternity.

Whatever their thoughts of these godless, primitive slaves, the sailors could only stare and marvel at the dance, mesmerised by the perfect harmony of the dancers and the sheer beauty of their movements. They were utterly oblivious to its significance. One or two of the crew had a vague foreboding that what they were witnessing was rather more than simple exercise, for the look in the women's eyes was bold and steely.

As the dance quickened and women stamped their feet to the ever-pulsating rhythm of the drums, the *obeah* darted forward towards the men, first short, uncertain runs, then longer steps, as if teasing and goading them to join the dance. The men played their part, initially disdainful of the woman's taunts, reluctant to yield to her provocation. Slowly but surely, however, they could not help themselves: their bodies succumbed to the rhythm and beckoning movements of this teasing woman.

Once she'd overcome their resistance, the lone dancer added song to the dance – a mournful wail that rose up from her very soul, spread like a cloud through the shrouds and flapping sails, across the surging sea and into the cloudless sky, echoing all the way back to Africa:

Down my cheeks the tears are falling,
Broken is my heart with grief,
Mangled my poor flesh from weeping.
Come, kind death, and give relief.

Born on Africa's golden coast,
Once I was as blessed as you,
Parents tender I could boast,
Husband dear and children too.

White men from afar did come,
Sailing over the ocean flood;
With their gold, cloth and gun
Bought my human flesh and blood.

The dirge was taken up by the female chorus, like Sirens calling sailors to their doom. Tears were falling from the grief-stricken women, touching the hearts of the shackled men across the deck. All at once, in low, husky voices, men took up the song, responding with their own refrain.

> *Driven by love of filthy gold,*
> *Men chained and bore us to the sea,*
> *Crammed us into the slave ship's hold*
> *Where many hundreds lie like me.*
>
> *Naked on a platform lying,*
> *Now we cross the tossing wave,*
> *Shrieking, moaning, fainting, crying,*
> *How many warriors dying brave?*
>
> *Putrid food they bring us nigh;*
> *Sick and sad we cannot eat.*
> *'The whip must cure!' they cry,*
> *As down our throats they force the meat.*

There was a brief pause before both sides started up again together. Their angry chant collided in mid-air, making all who heard it tremble. Although the crew did not understand a word, they sensed hatred in the ferocity of the song.

Driven like cattle to a fair,
See how they sell us, young and old.
Child from mother too they tear,
All for love of filthy gold!

Song and dance over, the *obeah* stood quite still, her right arm raised as if hurling a spear at some unseen prey. Everyone watched in silence. All at once, she gave a shout of triumph,

'We shall survive!'

To which the men responded loudly,

'Unnn!'

'We shall return!'

'Unnn!'

'Death to the slavers!'

'Unnn! Unnn! Unnn!'

This was too much for the onlookers. At the sight of the scantily-clad woman dancer and this tumultuous finale, they broke into spontaneous applause, punctuated by admiring shouts.

But the show wasn't quite over.

Amidst the clapping and shouting the *obeah*, beads of sweat rolling down her cheeks and chest, sang out some final words. It was as if she was giving her blessing to men and women alike.

'The weapon store is on the quarterdeck...'

'Unnn!'

'...opposite the officers' quarters.'

'*Unnn!*'

'We're chained at night between the two.'

Unnn!

As the days went by, more secrets were passed on.

'The Master-at-Arms has the armoury keys.'

'The red-haired overseer has the shackle keys.'

And so it went on, giving hope to all the slaves – and providing information.

Whenever Abena and Afi descended into the hellish bowels the ship, they did so with mixed feelings: dread of the nauseous stench and anticipation of their talk with Teiko. To the men about him, Teiko passed on messages from the women and, in turn, conveyed the men's questions and instructions to the sisters.

'We need a plan of the ship,' said Abena. 'We must get our hands on a ship's chart, or draw a sketch ourselves.'

'Can you steal pen, ink and paper?' asked Teiko doubtfully.

'Perhaps.'

That night, whispers passed to and fro among the women: how could they get their hands on materials to make a sketch? There was one possibility. One of the young Ashanti girls, Amakei, was responsible for cleaning the Captain's cabin. Although she was a year older than Abena, she was a timid, tearful, nervous sort of girl. It was too risky to entrust such a vital mission to her. Not if it meant rummaging through the Captain's desk, stealing keys, ink, pen and paper.

After long discussion, it was decided that Amakei would go down with a fever next morning and Abena would take her place.

Twenty-two

Mungo's first instinct was to run. Blindly. Anywhere. To put as much distance as possible between himself and the body. Don Jose's bloated face haunted his every step.

It was all *his* fault. He had as good as handed the murderers a dagger to slit the Spaniard's throat. Someone at the inn must have overheard talk of the black slave and the scrap of paper. They must have thought the slave was still alive and the sketch could damage their bounty business. So they'd murdered the Spaniard. Just as surely as they would slit Mungo's throat too...

His running feet had taken him past the Garrison Church, and out into the wide open spaces where the wiry grass of the common reached down to the sea. Apart from a lone beachcomber far out along the strand, there was no one in sight. No one to jump out of the shadows and crush his bones to dust. No one to creep up and stab him in the back. No one to slash off his head with a sharp cutlass.

He staggered to a halt, out of breath. As he sank down on a grassy mound, he loosened his collar to let the cold air mop up the sweat. While he was getting his breath back, he absent-mindedly drew patterns in the sand with the toe of a sandal.

When he'd recovered, he pulled his coat collar tight and set off again, treading down the stiff grass as he made for the high street. The grey cathedral dome guided his steps.

Before today he had never dared call on Mr Jeffs. But he had his address scribbled down – 'for emergencies', the brewer had said. *No. 2 St Thomas Street,* at the back of the cathedral.

From the hustle and bustle of carts and barrows, Mungo reckoned it must be around eight oclock, a reasonable hour to go knocking on decent folk's doors. They were supposed to need more beauty sleep than common folk – time to take a bath in their bathrooms, dress up in their dressing-rooms, take breakfast in their breakfast-rooms, dine in their dining-rooms, sit in their sitting-rooms...

It didn't take long to find No. 2. It was a tall, salmon-pink house on three floors, with a shiny black front door and grey smoke curling up from an orange chimney.

Mungo hesitated when faced with the heavy black knocker. Surely it wasn't intended for the likes of him. He would have preferred to tap on a back window or side door, or pass a message by way of a parlour-maid.

But since there wasn't an alleyway or tradesman's entrance, he had no choice. He had to climb up three steep steps and stand on tip-toe to reach the knocker with his fingertips. When he lifted the huge hammer and let it fall, he got a fright. A thunderclap echoed through the house and down the street, scaring pigeons up from the gutter.

Footsteps clip-clopped within, growing louder as they approached. Slowly, the great door opened and a stony-faced maid stared down at him. In the world of service, each and everyone had their place. The parlour-maid might be on the bottom rung of the servant ladder, but she was unmistakedly higher up than this guttersnipe standing three steps below her – the very steps she'd scrubbed clean that morning.

As she opened the door, the maid's expression changed from a polite smile to a scowl. She growled, 'Yeah? Wadyerwant?'

The maid's tone irritated Mungo; he'd come across hoity-toity skivvies at the inn, sent by the master for a jug of ale.

'I'm here to see Mr Jeffs,' said Mungo firmly, *'on a private matter.'*

The maid was taken aback. She was about to give this cheeky ragamuffin a piece of her mind, when a shout came from within. She swiftly pulled the door to, until just the red tip of her nose poked through the gap.

'State yer business or push off,' she said.

Mungo spoke to the red nose, stressing every word.

'Tell your master that Mungo from the stable is here, on a matter of life or death!'

The door banged shut and Mungo was left listening to the *clip-clop, clip-clop* dying away – into somewhere nice and warm, he bet, laid with plush carpets you'd sink into up to your knees.

He stood shivering on the bottom step, slapping his arms against his sides and blowing on his numb hands. Now and then he darted furtive glances towards both corners of the streets.

He was on the point of running off when the door suddenly swung inwards. There, taking up the entire doorway, was a beefy figure in carpet slippers. It was Jacob Jeffs, owner of the city's main brewery, purveyor of fine ales to the Royal Navy and a man of means. It was Mungo's drays which pulled his carts on special occasions.

Jacob Jeffs was a colourful character, often seen about town in stovepipe hat, black frock coat and trousers, with grey spats to protect his polished boots. If it weren't for his mutton-chop whiskers and bright waistcoats, you might have mistaken him for an undertaker.

Mr Jeffs was in the habit of patting his belly and boasting that his success was due to sampling his own stout. 'Stout by trade and stout by nature,' he'd boom out, with a twinkle in his eye.

He stared the boy up and down sternly before a look

of recognition lit up his face. A welcoming smile dimpled his ruddy cheeks.

'Hello, nipper,' he said loudly. 'Come on in. Come on in. Don't stand there cluttering up the pavement.'

Scraping his sandals on the iron grating beside the bottom step, Mungo climbed the stone steps. The hallway was dark and dingy. He shuffled after Mr Jeffs down an unlit, oak-panelled corridor with a bare floor below and a muddy brown ceiling above. The house smelt sweetly of port and floor polish.

The room Mr Jeffs led him to was gloomy, too. Its heavy, dark-green curtains were still drawn; the only light came from three candles in the centre of the mahogany table.

'Sit you down, boy,' said Mr Jeffs. 'First, a hot drink, then tell me all the news, eh?'

Without waiting for an answer, he rang a little brass bell. In response to the *ting-a-ling*, the clip-clop maid bustled in and planted herself before the master, head bent, arms behind her back. She stood sideways on to Mungo, keeping her eyes straight ahead, so as to shut him out.

'Bring us some hot milk, Molly.'

Molly bustled off. Then Mr Jeffs turned his watery eyes on Mungo and asked about his horses, life at the inn, the books he'd read lately.

It wasn't long before the jug of milk arrived on a silver tray. Molly put the tray down gently on the polished table-top and poured two mugs. Mr Jeffs dropped three lumps of sugar into his. Mungo helped himself to one.

When the hot milk trickled through Mungo's body, it thawed out the frozen words at the back of his throat. 'I'm right grateful, Mr Jeffs, for you asking me in,' he said.

The master brushed this aside with a wave of his hand and glanced at the ticking clock on the sideboard.

'Right, lad, I've seventeen minutes. Let's have it.'

Mungo had to share his troubles with someone. Mr Jeffs was the only person in the world who could help him.

He told him everything.

In the heavy silence that followed, Mungo heard his own heart thumping and the scratching of whiskers. It reminded him of the rasping noise hogs make when scratching their backs against the sty wall.

When at last the brewer spoke, the sound made Mungo jump.

'Jumping Jehosephat!'

He repeated this a few times while mulling over the tale. Jacob Jeffs prided himself on being a man of action, a decisive man.

'Right, lad, this is what we'll do.'

The master poured himself another mug of milk and rocked back in his chair, blinked his eyes and spoke.

'You can't stay here – or we'll all wake up with our

throats cut! But where will you go?'

He rubbed his chin between his side whiskers and drummed stubby orange fingers on a mustard belly.

'You'll only be safe out of harm's way, right? Now, here's the plan. I'm supplying victuals to a privateer, *The Adventure Galley*. She's sailing shortly for the Caribbean, hired by King William himself to carry cargo from our colonies. I know the Captain, a God-fearing man by the name of Kidd. He's taking on crew right now. I know he needs a cabin boy. His last one went overboard on the trip across. I'll put in a word for you.'

'What about Josh and Bessie, sir?' said Mungo, looking at his feet. 'You won't forget to feed and water them properly, will you?

A twinkle came into the brewer's pale blue eyes.

'Can't have my old nags croaking, now, can I? No, no, I give you my word as a gentleman – they'll be well cared for.'

Twenty-three

An hour later Mungo and Mr Jeffs were climbing the gangplank to *The Adventure Galley*. A smartly dressed officer in the dark blue uniform of the Royal Navy awaited them on deck.

'Good morning, sirs,' he said politely. 'Captain's awaiting you in his cabin. This way, please.'

The tall officer led the way to steps up to the quarter deck where, between wheel and gangway, stood a low structure like a lean-to shed – with portholes along both sides.

At a smart rap from the escort, a deep voice within called, 'Come,' and the officer opened the door. With a quick salute, he stepped back and ushered the two visitors inside.

If Mungo was mildly disappointed by the modest exterior, he was pleasantly surprised by the homeliness of Captain Kidd's cabin. It was more like a scholar's study than a naval commander's room. Leather-bound books lined the walls, a medicine chest stood in one corner at the head of a curtained bunk. Beneath one porthole, two huge books lay open – the ship's journal and the Captain's diary.

Mungo had read about those in the Admiralty books

at the inn. A quill pen and inkwell were fastened securely between brass rails – to keep them from spilling out in a storm. The room was spotless and the boy wondered what sort of person this Captain Kidd could be.

A large fleshy man of about fifty was sitting at an almost bare desk facing the door. He was poring intently over a map.

If Mungo's companion took pride in being colourful, and as whiskery as an old yard broom, Captain Kidd looked the very image of the Scottish minister whose son he was. The only colour about him was in his smooth purple cheeks and nose. They contrasted starkly with the grey, shoulder-length wig, black frock-coat, white ruffed shirt and silk muffler at the throat. Mungo observed the high shiny forehead, bushy black eyebrows and wide flared nostrils. When he looked up, the boy was able to complete the picture: cold, piercing eyes, a thin upper lip above a full lower one, and an odd-shaped chin, rather like the knob end of a walking-stick.

'Captain Kidd,' began the brewer, 'I've brought you a new cabin boy. I can vouch for him myself.'

If Mungo thought the Captain disdainful, he was mistaken. William Kidd was one of the shrewdest judges of character he was ever likely to meet. He hand-picked every man of his crew, and he was now sizing up the youngster before him.

'Name?' he suddenly barked, making Mungo jump.

'Mungo – Mungo Mullins, sir,' he stuttered.

'Age?'

'Twelve.'

'You're awfully wee for twelve.'

'I'm as tough as teak, sir. I can do the work of any grown man.'

'Oh, can you now? Parents?'

'Drowned at sea, sir. When I was six. I've made my own way since then.'

'Previous work?'

'Handyman: cleaning, washing, serving, scrubbing, unloading. Spice Island Inn. Seven days a week, dawn to midnight.'

'Knowledge of the sea?'

'Only what I've read in books, sir.'

The bushy black eyebrows rose half an inch.

'So you can read?'

'And write, sir.'

For the first time the Captain looked him full in the face. Mungo held his gaze for a minute before the next words came.

'You'll do, laddie.'

Turning to the brewer, his face as flat as stale beer, he muttered, 'Ye didna say he was as measly as watered-down gruel.'

Before Mr Jeffs could reply, Kidd stood up and offered a large hand to the brewer.

'Done,' was all he said, as if clinching a deal.

To the new cabin boy, he said sternly, 'Right, laddie, report for duty tomorrow.'

He sat down and returned to his maps.

Interview over, the brewer and the ship's new cabin boy turned to go. The officer waiting outside escorted them back to the quay, where they climbed into the carriage and rattled off towards Queen Street.

With a sigh of relief, Mr Jeffs said, 'Dry old stick, isn't he? Said to be a good captain, though. So, young Mungo, you've passed the test. If Kidd says you'll do, that's as much praise as you'll ever prise out of him. Thank God you're off my hands now.'

Mungo hardly heard. He was craning his neck to get a last glimpse of the black and gold brig towering over the ships around her. It was the most magnificent vessel he'd ever seen. He could imagine how grand she'd look in full sail, ploughing through the waves. And to think Master Mullins was now one of her crew...

Twenty-four

When Abena reported for duty to Captain Bibby, he noticed nothing amiss: all black girls looked the same to him. After his customary outburst of curses in a language Abena didn't understand, but well knew the meaning of, the Captain left her to it. Amakei had told her the routine: make up the bunk, scrub the bare boards, polish the cutlery, clean the porthole and dust every surface spotlessly clean, spick and span.

Once she was alone, however, instead of reaching for her duster, Abena went to the cabin door and peered out. Seeing no one around, she pulled the door to and set to work. It didn't take long to locate what she was seeking. There, on a small oak table beneath the porthole, next to various charts and the ship's log, were a quill pen stuck in its holder and a squat bottle of ink.

As luck would have it, the desk drawer was unlocked. Pulling it open, she came upon the third object of her hunt: a pile of creamy parchment.

If she were to steal the pen and ink from the Captain's desk, there would be hell to pay. What was worse, the blame would fall on poor Amakei... The Captain would have no hesitation in feeding her to the sharks.

Despite searching the small cabin, she found no sign of other writing utensils. She'd have to be content with a few sheets of paper taken from the desk. Swiftly she snatched up four sheets, thrust them down her shirt and shut the drawer.

Just in time. The door flew open and in stormed the Captain, clearly in a rage about something: the weather, lack of a breeze, sloppy crew, insolent slaves – who knows? It took little for him to lose his temper. Now, alone with the girl in his cabin, he took his rage out on her, knocking her to the floor with his fist and kicking her as she lay there writhing. Only the bo'sun's shouts halted the assault.

When he'd gone, she pulled herself to her feet, aching all over. As best she could, she set about her cleaning tasks, before the Captain returned. If he were to have her whipped, he'd rip the shirt off her back and soon discover the stolen parchment. That would be the end of her... and of the mutiny.

Luckily for Abena, the Captain was now busy on the bridge, staring at the horizon and shouting up to the look-out in the crow's nest. Something was agitating the sailors as they gazed out across the sea.

Abena limped from the cabin, her left eye closed, her nose bleeding, her arms and legs covered in cuts and bruises. A light of triumph gleamed in her one good eye. She had fulfilled part of her assignment.

But what use was paper without pen and ink?

None of the crew paid any attention to the women as they gathered about Abena. Instead, the *obeah* did what she could to patch Abena up with strips of cloth torn from cleaning rags, and a thick black ointment 'borrowed' from the surgeon's stock of cure-alls.

While she was being treated, Abena revealed her four sheets of paper. There were more than a few downcast faces: what good was mere paper? Even the *obeah* voiced her doubts.

'You're a brave girl. But without ink and pen the paper is useless. We'll have to scrap the plan.'

'No!'

It was timid Amakei who'd spoken, taking everyone by surprise.

'Abena has taken a beating meant for me. We mustn't let her down. I have an idea.'

As all eyes turned to the girl, she dropped her eyes in confusion. Her next words were so quiet, they had to strain their ears to catch them.

'My father was a scribe for the *oba*. He recorded our people's history as well as births and deaths. He wrote it all with a pen made from a wild duck feather...'

A loud snort from an older woman interrupted her.

'There aren't any wild ducks on the ocean!'

The girl's eyes filled with tears. It was Abena who broke the silence.

'True, we have no ducks... But we do have gulls and petrels.'

'Do you have a catapult to shoot them down?'

Abena shook her head, but she wasn't defeated.

'Now and again a bird flies blindly into the sails or drops exhausted on to the deck. If we keep looking, we might find a dead bird in the debris.'

The women still had doubts.

'Say we were to find a seabird,' one said, ' and made a pen from its feathers, what would we use for ink? You can't risk raiding the Captain's stores again.

'I know what we can use.'

It was Amakei's tremulous voice again.

'My father was headman and could read and write. When he wrote to the king, he made his own ink. He'd ask me to bring him beetles which I ground to a black powder and bound together with egg yolk.'

'We've plenty of beetles, that's for sure,' said someone. 'But eggs don't drop out of the sky, do they?'

'No, but something else does!' said Amakei. 'Once my father used chicken droppings. They smelt awful. But the ink worked.'

Now the *obeah* stepped in.

'We're not short of bird droppings,' she said. 'Right, let's give it a try.'

She detailed groups of women to their tasks: one for beetles, one for bird droppings and one for dead birds. The first two were in plentiful supply, the last was hard to find. But they were in luck. A stormy petrel was found in the bowsprit, tangled up in a coil of rope.

They set to work. While Amakei mixed crushed beetle juice and powder with the scraped-up bird droppings, another girl plucked feathers from the petrel's tail.

When all was ready, the women huddled about Abena as she dipped a quill pen into the mixture and tried it out, first on the back of her hand, then on the precious paper. Then she drew a rough sketch of their quarters between decks, showing the weapon store and the officers' cabins.

On the second sheet she drew the exact location of the Captain's cabin on the quarter deck, with a plan of the interior: desk, bunk, charts, porthole.

The third sketch indicated the galley and quarters of the other hands on the half deck: where they slung their hammocks, ate their food and manned the ship's six cannon.

Her drawings done, Abena looked up to the *obeah*. 'What shall I do with the last sheet?' she asked

The obeah shrugged her shoulders. Then an idea came to her.

'Abena, you and your sister have been down to the hold. You've seen how many slaves are kept there, shackled together, with no space to move. It's the only part of the ship you haven't sketched. Who knows? It might come in handy.'

Abena dipped a third quill into the fast-hardening

mess and drew the scene below decks as accurately as she could recall it. Judging by the number of men brought up for exercise, the women agreed there had to be getting on for seven or eight hundred bodies packed tightly together.

Abena's last sketch turned out better than the rest, since the 'ink' didn't run or make splodgy blots on the paper. She felt quite proud of her four sketches, and added her name to the fourth.

Now came the next task: to smuggle the ship's layout to the men below. Once again, Abena, with her sister Afi, was to be the go-between. However, there would be no time that day. Already, all hands were dashing about the deck, cleaning muskets and manning the cannons on the half deck. Captain Bibby was standing on the forecastle deck beside the capstan, staring intently ahead. The look-out had passed on disturbing news.

'Ship on starboard bow!'

Bibby was puzzled. He stood, legs apart, on the forecastle deck beside the capstain, staring intently ahead. It was probably another slaver blown off course on the first leg of its trip to Africa. No danger to the *Sea Venture*. But the look-out warned otherwise.

'Heading our way, Captain!'

'What the devil!' muttered Bibby. 'Not another pirate victim…'

But it wasn't a pirate victim. It was pirates!

Twenty-five

In the distance, sailing towards them, was a ship flying the Jolly Roger. As it hove into view, the crew saw with alarm that it was bristling with cannon.

The Captain knew his *Sea Venture* was no match for such a well-armed frigate; he could only put up a token defence before surrendering. With any luck, he might bargain his way out of trouble by giving up part of his black cargo.

Worse news was to come as the look-out's yell flew down on the breeze:

'She's the *Queen Anne's Revenge*, Cap'n.'

Bibby's face went as grey as his patched-up sails.

'That's Blackbeard's flagship!' he muttered. 'We're done for!'

The odds were stacked against them. The pirate frigate was armed with forty cannon and built for combat. The *Sea Venture* was a slaver brig, no more than a creaking old tub; normally slavers did twenty three-way trips: Bristol – Gold Coast – West Indies and back home again. By then, they were fit only for the breakers' yard. And the *Sea Venture* was on her twenty-third voyage. Her six cannon were intended more to impress natives than to repel borders.

Bibby did his best to skirt the bigger ship, which was low in the water and making heavy weather through the waves. But with the wind against her, the brig couldn't tack swiftly enough. As she came within a hundred yards of the frigate, the Captain saw he had no option but to stand and fight.

'Right, men,' his voice rang out. 'You know the drill: attack from the stern to avoid a broadside attack.'

The crew scurried to their posts: heavy gunners down to the cannon, light gunners up on deck and in the rigging, muskets and flintlocks at the ready. The rest would have to rely on their cutlasses.

To his chief gunner in the bows, Bibby yelled, 'Keep your powder dry, Mister Lee. When we come in close, take aim at the ropes holding her sails. Cut through them, and they'll tumble about their heads.'

'Tom! Jeremiah!' he shouted to two young crewmen. 'Dive overboard and jam her rudder so she can't veer about and ram us amidships.'

The Captain had words, too, for the cutlass-wielding boarding party lined up on deck:

'Follow me as we go alongside. Our chief weapons are speed and surprise. We can't afford to trade shots.'

It wasn't long before the frigate loomed large no more than twenty yards away. By contrast with the patched-up *Sea Venture*, she was a splendid sight as she ploughed through the waves; her high stern was ornately carved and above the bridge could be seen the name, *Queen Anne's Revenge,* in gold letters. The Captain's cabin was a much grander affair than Bibby's, with two large green-tinted windows on either side of the stern.

As the pirate ship came ever closer, Abena, who alone of the slaves was kept on deck to help, saw the sun glinting on brass cannon poking out like pig snouts. She counted the guns gleaming wickedly off the sunlit sea.

Her gaze swept over the ship until it settled on a terrifying sight. She'd seen some ugly demons among the Red Faces, but this was the most frightening of them all. Standing on the bridge was a giant of a man with the wildest features she'd ever clapped eyes on. A mass of tangled black hair covered most of his face and spread out and down, so that all she could make out were two staring eyes, a hooked nose and a low forehead.

At first she took the figure to be a gorilla brought from the jungle to fight or scare the enemy. Yet from somewhere in the midst of the coal-black hair issued noises more akin to those of red-faced humans than of wild animals.

And then there were its clothes... Perched like a carrion crow on the shaggy head was a black, three-cornered hat. But it was the sight beneath the hat that convinced her this was a demon. Alongside the ears were slow-burning fuses sparkling and spluttering –

the whole shaggy head seemed to be on fire!

Slung across the creature's chest were six pistols and in each hand was a huge cutlass. Although it walked upright, the demon had dressed itself in a blue frock coat that fell to its ankles.

From the scared mutterings of the *Sea Venture* crew, it seemed they feared the monster as much as she did.

Far quicker than Captain Bibby had anticipated, the two ships came together broadside on – for the breeze had suddenly got up, filling the frigate's billowing sails and driving her headlong towards her prey. It was too late for gunners to fire their cannon.

The battle was over almost before it had begun. With several of his crew, the burning demon leapt over the bows, hurling smoke bombs and slashing right and left. Fearing for his life and his ship, Captain Bibby surrendered, handing the ship over to Captain Edward Teach – otherwise known as Blackbeard the Pirate.

If Bibby and his crew had treated the slaves like caged animals, what were they to expect from this blood-thirsty band of brigands?

But Blackbeard had no interest in slaves. He dared not risk landing a human cargo in port for fear of being caught and strung up along with his crew. A large bounty was on his head, and merchantmen were everywhere on the look-out for him. So when the rum-sodden pirate chief discovered he'd captured a slaver, he ranted and raved like one demented, dancing up and down and hitting out in all directions. He blamed everyone but himself.

Abena thought he'd scuttle the ship and throw them all into the sea – black, pink, brown, red alike. But he decided to make the best of a bad job and salvage what he could from the cargo and provisions.

'Show me your merchandise!' he ordered.

When they led him down into the hold, even Blackbeard, the scruffiest, dirtiest captain on the high seas, was shocked. The stench fought its way through the tangled bush into his nostrils and mouth. But it was the sight in the dim light of the lower deck that made him blink in astonishment. It reminded him of a honey pot swarming with black ants – hundreds and hundreds of them, wherever you looked, with barely space between their bodies.

Swiftly beating a retreat, he came up for air and made a quick decision.

'Captain, we're both old salts, and you know the law of the high seas. No prey, no pay. My men expect booty. If they don't get it, they'll mutiny. Here are my demands.'

He read out a list.

'Medicine chest, spare tackle, candles, rope and oakum. And as much bread and meat from the stores as I can carry. I'm not a hard man...'

He guffawed into his beard.

'...I'll leave you enough to last out the voyage.

For the crew, that is. God knows what you'll feed your slaves on. They'll probably eat each other, savages that they are.'

To one of his crew, he bawled, 'Fetch me fifty of the slaves – the fittest and strongest you can find. We could do with extra hands. Compared with your hell-hole of a ship, Captain, the poor savages will think they've landed in heaven!'

As scores of slaves emerged, blinking, into the sunlight, Abena was both glad and dismayed to see Teiko and her brother Kwame. They exchanged anxious glances as the men's shackles were removed, uncertain of their fate.

While the slaves were being transferred to the frigate, Blackbeard took a last look round for anything else he could plunder. His gaze lighted on the group of scantily-clad girls and women cowering about the foremast. Wielding a bottle of brandy, he let out a deafening belch and gestured towards the women. A low rumble, like approaching thunder, came from the black hole amid his matted foliage.

'Shiver me timbers! Here's fun and games for me and me lads!'

Although the women didn't understand his words, the meaning was clear enough from the leer in his eye and the vile gestures of his hands. Striding over to Abena and the other trembling females, he began pinching and prodding them, before roughly yanking out those he fancied. His taste was obviously for older women – or perhaps he felt the younger girls wouldn't survive rough handling by drunken pirates.

While the more mature women, including their chief, the *obeah*, were flung to one side, Abena and her sister Afi clung tightly to their mother, trying to shield her from the monster's clutches. To their relief, the pirate passed over her.

The obeah whispered, just loud enough for Abena to hear, 'Give me the last sketch, the one of the hold. Who knows, maybe I can make something of it? Use the other three as best you can.' And then she hissed, 'Remember. We *shall* survive! We *shall* return! If not us, then our children, our children's children, or their children…'

Thrusting the sketch into her loincloth, she went off with the chosen band of women. Now all that remained were Abena, Afi and their mother and nine other girls.

Twenty-six

The slaves' plan to take over the ship was now in ruins. Without Teiko's contact with the men and the *obeah*'s guidance, Abena saw no hope of a revolt. From now on their aim would be simply to survive.

If the first part of the voyage had been torment, now began an unimaginably wretched time. The barbarism of Blackbeard's pirates made the Captain and crew think they'd been too lenient with the slaves.

Not only that. The *Sea Venture* had been left with a little meat, bread as hard as nails and pitted with green mould, and tack biscuits so full of weevils, they actually moved as if on legs. Worse still, there was hardly any water.

Nor was there any ointment and medicine left to treat sores and fevers. Open wounds on crew and slaves festered; fevers would be left to rage until the patient died or got better. There was nothing to stop scurvy eating into red and brown flesh alike.

The crew had no raw rum to dull the pain of their empty stomachs, scurvy and their running sores. More ominously for the Captain, there was no rum to divert their attention from thoughts of mutiny.

Captain Bibby made a tough decision. Given

favourable winds, they faced another thirty days before making port. At worst, the journey would take another six weeks. Fortunately, there was a smell of rain in the air and the sky was charged with electric clouds, promising torrents of rain. At least that would refill the water barrels.

But provisions were barely enough to feed the crew and the surviving slaves. The Captain had lost sixty slaves through illness and another fifty to Blackbeard; there still remained some six hundred mouths to feed. Bibby's choice was simple: either he could starve all his slaves to death or he could ditch the sick, leaving the rest to survive as best they could. Even then, they would be walking skeletons by the time he made port and unlikely to fetch a decent price.

If the slaves were a problem, so were his rebellious crew. He could see in their eyes that it wouldn't take much for a mutiny to break out. They might not be as squeamish as he was about cutting up Africans and boiling their meat to survive.

The ship rode out the breaking storm, but the tail of a hurricane swept them before it at such a rapid rate of knots, they covered a distance in two days that would normally have taken twenty. The only trouble was – they'd gone aft instead of for'ard.

The dozen female slaves had ridden out the storm. The men weren't so lucky: at least a hundred had either starved or stifled to death. Abena watched sadly as their bodies were tossed into the sea, sometimes four at a time, shackled to one another.

In his cabin Bibby sat at his desk, compass in hand, poring over the charts and trying to work out days and miles to land. If he were to steer as the crow flies to Jamaica, there would hardly be a slave left alive by the time they arrived.

With a sigh, he pushed aside the charts, dipped his pen into the ink and started to write in the ship's log.

> *'Sixteenth of November in the Year of our Lord, 1729.*
>
> *Fifteen Crew and ninety-eight Negroes dead from Starvation and Suffocation. I, Uriah Bibby, Master of His Majesty's Ship, the Sea Venture, committed their Bodies to the Sea and (in the Case of Christian Sailors) their Souls to the Almighty.*
>
> *For Purposes of an Insurance of Thirty Pounds per Slave, I testify that a Total of 98 (Ninety Eight) of the Negro Merchandise had to be jettisoned...'*

All at once, he heard a shout from the mainsail top. 'Land ahoy! Starboard bow.'

He dropped the pen and breathed a sigh of relief. By his reckoning, they could be in sight of the islands of the Bahamas. To make Jamaica, they would have to steer a course between Cuba and Hispaniola – a matter of days given fair winds and a safe passage. And he could call in at an island to stock up with supplies. But he wasn't counting his chickens... Many's the slaver that had come to grief in the last few days of the Middle Passage.

Captain Bibby prided himself on running a tidy ship. So he was determined to have the decks spick and span, as regulations prescribed, just in case some nosy colonial inspector came on board. When he appeared on deck, he could see the change that had come over his men. Their bloodshot eyes shone with renewed hope; a few were humming or whistling to themselves, and all had a jauntier look about them.

'Look lively, you men!' he hollered. 'Swab down the decks with water and vinegar. Bring up the slaves, unlock their shackles. Let them get fresh air into their lungs. Clean them up as best you can. Then send the women below to clear out the hold. Get to it!'

The sight of land produced mixed feelings in Abena. What fate awaited them now? Were the stories true, that they would be eaten by the Red Faces? Or would they be harnessed to carts and ploughs, like oxen or buffalo?

Whatever was to come, it would be no better than what had gone before.

Twenty-seven

Mr Jeffs was too scared of waking up with his throat cut to let Mungo spend the night under his roof, so the boy slept rough that night, in a ditch behind Garrison Church. When he went to report for duty next day, Mr Jeffs accompanied him to the quayside.

He had kitted the boy out with a pair of sturdy boots, black linen trousers, a clean white shirt and a padded jacket. True, the jacket and breeches were rather baggy. 'But you'll grow into them,' was his cheery comment.

It was a crisp sunny morning with a smooth bottle-green sea and a few wispy clouds in the sky. A straggly line of would-be hands stretched from the quay all the way up to the Captain's cabin. Kidd was busy selecting his men.

'With any luck,' thought Mungo, 'he'll weed out any evil-looking brigands like Blood and Weasel – *if* they've got wind of my sea-going plans.'

'Now then, lad,' said Mr Jeffs on parting. 'You'll be out of harm's way on the high seas. And it'll do you a power of good – put a blush on those pasty cheeks and hair on your chest. When you return, you'll be a big, strapping sailor, and all this palaver will have blown over.'

Mungo smiled gratefully. He owed much to this kindly man.

'You've saved my bacon, sir,' he said warmly. 'I'm in your debt. I don't know how to thank you…'

Mr Jeffs waved away the thanks.

'One last word,' he said, gripping the boy's hand. 'Don't cross Kidd. He'll treat you fair and square. But he's got a foul temper, especially when the drink's inside him. Now, fare ye well, Master Mullins. God be with you.'

'Thank you, sir. Thank you.'

Waving, he squeezed past the queue and clambered up on deck.

'Master Mullins!'

Amidst all the hubbub, Mungo barely recognised the unfamiliar name. It was only when the man bellowed in his ear that he realised – *he* was Master Mullins!

'Have you got cloth ears, lad?'

'Sorry, sir,' Mungo mumbled.

'I'm the ship's bo'sun, Thomas Mace,' the man said. 'Come with me. I'm to show you the ropes – since it's your first time at sea. Then you're to put your mark to the Articles. Come on, jump to it!'

As Mungo fell in behind him, he wondered what Articles were. Put his mark on them indeed! Still, the bo'sun wouldn't expect a cabin boy to read and write.

The bo'sun hadn't gone twenty paces before halting amidships. At eye level was a stiff yellow parchment nailed to the mast. It bore Captain Kidd's signature and a royal seal at the bottom.

'*CREW'S RIGHTS AND DUTIES,*' the bo'sun read out.

Mungo guessed these were the Articles. He read out the list before the bo'sun could continue.

> *Everyone must obey Orders.*
>
> *Anyone who is lazy or who fails to do his Duty shall be fined and forfeit his Pay.*
>
> *Anyone found stealing from a Shipmate shall have his Ears and Nose slit open and be set ashore.*
>
> *Gambling with Cards or Dice for Money is forbidden.*
>
> *The Punishment for fighting is forty Lashes with the Cat O' Nine Tails.*
>
> *One Tot of Rum shall be issued to each Crew Member every Day.*

Although Mungo stumbled over a few words, like 'Gambling' and 'Punishment', the officer was impressed.

'No seaman would sail without such a contract,' Mr Mace explained. 'They know how important discipline is on a long voyage. Brawls, mutiny and desertion are common on other ships. But Captain Kidd won't tolerate indiscipline on his ship. Now, put your name to the Articles.'

Beside the mast was an upturned wooden box on which was pinned a sheet with some twenty names or crosses alongside printed names. Mungo dipped the quill pen into an inkwell and signed his name: *Master Mungo Mullins.*

He had signed on! Now he was a sailor in the King's Navy.

'Right, follow me down below,' ordered Mr Mace.

Twenty-eight

Mungo was surprised at how much space there was below deck – first on the half deck and then on the lower deck, where the cannons were. The wooden floors were spick and span, the brass cannon had had their muzzles cleaned and cannon balls polished until they gleamed like a fiery sun.

He saw no sign of sleeping or eating places. Evidently the men ate and slept on the bare boards. Down in the hold Mister Mace showed him first the armoury, full of muskets tied down with rope, then the food stores – salted beef, stacks of biscuits, rum kegs, fresh-water butts, barrels of pickled apples and cabbage.

'That'll have to do us till we take on fresh supplies,' he said with a shrug. 'By then, a few drowned rats will have flavoured the water, the biscuits will be crawling with weevils, and the beef'll stink to high heaven. Still, there's always the rum to take the edge off your appetite.'

Mungo screwed up his nose.

'There's a brick-well on deck to catch the rain – but that doesn't go far with a hundred parched throats,' the bo'sun said.

'What exactly does a cabin boy do?' Mungo ventured to ask.

'Do?' Mr Mace said with a laugh. 'Whatever the Captain says: serve him his grub, tidy up his quarters, pour his rum, be at his beck and call. And when he doesn't need you, you shin up the rigging, scrub the decks, mend the sails, obey everyone's command.'

Mungo was beginning to wonder whether this could be worse than Spice Island.

'Most of us started out as cabin boys,' said the bo'sun, seeing his anxious look. 'We learned our trade the hard way. Then we graduated to deck hands: climbing the rigging, taking in jib and sails, scrubbing the decks clean of blood and salt, hauling on the anchor chain and hawser, sweating our guts out to make the grade. Stick at it, lad, and, who knows, you might make it to bo'sun one of these days.'

'Aye-aye, sir,' muttered Mungo.

Mr Mace led the new cabin boy to the galley where the men's food was cooked, right above the stores.

'Home sweet home, Master Mullins,' he said, pointing inside the low-ceilinged kitchen. 'Our last lad – God rest his soul – used to grab forty winks under the table over there by the wall. It's a bit cramped, but it's dry and warm beside the ovens.'

He turned to go.

'Now, young fellow, shake yourself down, then report to Captain Kidd for sailing orders.'

He left Mungo to explore the new quarters.

'So,' Mungo sighed, 'lesson one: cabin boys have no cabin.'

Having put his kitbag under the table and his purse inside his shirt beside the sketch, Mungo made his way to the Captain's cabin for sailing orders. Once again he had to squeeze past the queue of sailors, some of whom roundly cursed him.

He stood silently to one side, waiting for the Captain to notice him.

Kidd barely glanced up from his desk. Mungo thought he hadn't spotted him; but the Captain suddenly waved a hand brusquely in his direction, snapping, 'Get out of my light, damn you! Stand over by the bunk.'

Hastily, Mungo stepped three paces away from the porthole.

The bushy-bearded quartermaster was shepherding a line of likely Jack Tars before the Captain, four at a time.

'Name? Age? Trade?' he rapped out.

Kidd gave each a cursory glance, as if bored with the whole procedure.

'Adam Goss... 18... carpenter.'

'Aye.'

'Billy Watkins... 22... ship's cook.'

'Aye.'

'Rob Birdson... 27... gunner's mate.'

'Aye.'

'William Blood... 36... gunner.'

'Aye.'

Mungo froze with fear at the man's name.

Kidd stared at the man for a full minute, then nodded slowly.

'Have you read the Articles?' he asked the four men.

They nodded.

'Right. Dismissed. Next!'

As the next four men were herded into the cabin, Kidd beckoned to the new cabin boy.

'What do you make of them?'

What was Mungo to say? Blood's presence and cruel grin had scared him stiff.

'Decent sorts, sir,' he said... 'Only, the gunner, Blood – he struck me as a bit shifty.'

'Aye, good. I like an honest view,' Kidd said, slapping the desk with one hand. 'Keep an eye on him for me.'

Mungo didn't like the sound of that. Did the Captain really expect his cabin boy to spy for him? Was he to be the Captain's eyes and ears about the ship? No wonder the last cabin boy hadn't survived the trip. No one liked spies.

'Aye-aye, sir,' he murmured.

The parade continued, with a few candidates falling foul of the Captain's eye. Among the recruits were a dozen or more brought on board by crimps – men whose profession it was to ply a likely lad with booze, then, when he was too drunk to resist, to carry him on board as a 'recruit'. Often he'd wake up out to sea. But that wasn't Kidd's way; he needed to scrutinise every man Jack of his crew.

By mid-afternoon, fifty men had signed on. That made a total crew of eighty, including those who'd come over from the colonies.

On the morning of 24 November 1729, the ship weighed anchor, its chain grinding round the windlass. With the square sails billowing from the mast tops, *The Adventure Galley* sailed from Sallyport into the open sea.

She kept close to the wind and fairly skimmed over the Solent, round the Isle of Wight and out into the open sea. The brig was heading for Jamaica on the first leg of her voyage – to collect further orders from the island's Governor, Lord Belmont.

Twenty-nine

The Captain was so busy breaking in the new crew that he had no time for the new cabin boy.

'Awa' ye gang till I need ye,' he said gruffly.

So Mungo was free to enjoy the sights: the Needles rocks disappearing astern (he recalled sadly that this was the spot where his parents had drowned), the patched-up sails flapping loudly in the breeze, sailors rushing to and fro, climbing the rigging and tugging on ropes. He watched the Captain standing on the bridge, bellowing orders.

'Trim the mainsail.' 'More tack on the jib.' 'Look lively, you men.'

Mungo felt so happy with the wind on his cheeks, tasting the salt spray, gazing up at the cloudless blue sky. If this is what going to sea was all about, he must have the briny in his blood. If only Don Jose could see him now, as free as the squawking seagulls dipping and diving in their wake.

'*Vaja con dios*, Mungo – God be with you,' he would have said.

Thoughts of the Spaniard made Mungo sad. He started to shiver. It was now late afternoon and turning chilly. He needed his coat. Evidently cabin boys didn't rate a uniform, not even a hat. He turned away from the ship's rail and climbed backwards down the steep steps to the galley. Already the two cooks were hard at work preparing an evening meal for eighty hungry mouths – no mean task when there wasn't room enough to swing a cat.

The food was likely to be the freshest they were to eat on the entire voyage. What it would taste like after a few weeks at sea didn't bear thinking about.

Not wishing to disturb his new shipmates, Mungo edged round the galley wall and dived beneath the table. Above him, the man he remembered as Billy Watkins was kneading a great grey-yellow lump of dough on the floury table, while an older man was chopping up chunks of meat and dropping them into a tall tureen of boiling water.

If it was chilly up top, down in the galley it was baking hot. Both men were soaking wet and Billy's sweat was dripping like a leaky tap into the dough.

Catching sight of Mungo watching him, he said with a chuckle, 'Saves adding salt and water.'

The older man called out, 'How do, shipmate. Don't mind him. I put more than good honest sweat into this 'ere stew – makes it tastier. What's your name, lad?'

'I'm Master Mungo Mullins, sir.'

''Old hard, matey. You only call officers 'Sir' – got it? I'm James Jessup. This here's Billy Watkins.'

Billy thrust a soft white hand below the table-top, and Mungo shook it politely.

'First time out, Master Mullins?' asked Billy.

'Yes, but I've always wanted to go to sea.'

'You've a lot to learn, lad. Seafaring's a tough old mistress. Don't your parents mind?'

'They're dead, drowned at sea.'

The two cooks exchanged anxious glances. Like all mariners, they were deeply superstitious and believed in good and bad omens. Did this boy bring bad luck?

Mungo thought it time to go on deck. As he was leaving the galley, Billy called him back.

'The Captain's up at the wheel. Better take him his rum. If he don't get it, there's no telling what he'll do. But mark my words: steer well clear of him when the grog's inside him.'

Mungo took the mug of rum and, pulling himself up with one hand and holding the mug steady with the other, clambered up the steps.

Thirty

A full moon shone down, laying a broad carpet of rippling light upon the sea, as if showing the way. But Captain Kidd was keeping a keen weather eye on a thick bank of cloud climbing up the heavens. In half an hour it would swallow up the moon and most of the stars.

He took the rum from Mungo with a grunt, muttering, 'See – Heaven's light is our guide.'

Mungo well knew that ships sailed by the stars. So it took a skilled Captain to set the correct course under a cloudy sky.

Kidd was plainly ill at ease. He kept sniffing the air and licking the index finger of his right hand, holding it up to the wind. He studied the racing billows fore and aft, and was glancing up to measure the fast-closing gap between moon and cloud.

The boy recalled the old sailor's saying: *Red sky at night, sailor's delight*. And as he looked towards the horizon, he saw nothing but violet and black, like the entrance to Hell's cavern.

'Aye, we're in for a bumpy ride,' murmured the Captain. "'Tis a bad omen, first night out, Master Mullins. Go fetch the bo'sun, then tell the men to batten down the hatches and stores; have them report to me on deck double quick.'

Mungo ran off and bumped into Mister Mace at the top of the ladder. After passing on the Captain's message, he hurried below. On the half deck, where most of the crew were downing their supper, he piped up, 'Captain says to batten down the hatches and stores, and to report to him on deck.'

Most gobbled down their remaining stew and bread, then rushed off to do the Captain's bidding. But two sat tight, as if they hadn't heard. Mungo thought he'd better repeat the message for their benefit. So he approached the men and started to say 'Captain says...'

One of the men banged down his square tray and snarled, 'Who are you to give orders, pipsqueak? Sling yer hook! Go tell your Captain Kidd to batten down his lip!'

Mungo recognised him instantly, with his black eye patch and weasel face.

'I finish my supper in my own good time,' the man continued. 'Then I take my tot of rum. We're fighting men, gunners, not monkeys who swing on the rigging. Tell that to your skipper.'

His mate growled in agreement.

Mungo quickly turned away. So Blood and Weasel knew he was on board – otherwise why were they there?

One thing was for sure: there was no escape on

the ocean wave. But would they dare touch him with Captain Kidd around?

By the time Mungo surfaced, the first heavy drops of rain were falling. The bo'sun was at the wheel, while the Captain was standing on the bridge, yelling orders right, left and centre, twisting his head to port and starboard so that everyone could hear him. Men were shimmying up the shrouds, using the ratlines as ladders, right up to the mizzen top, desperately trying to untangle the topsail. If the storm broke before the topsail was freed, the ship might keel over and they'd all be feeding the fishes.

It was not long before a raging squall overtook them, the waves rearing their white heads. Blinding rain teemed down, the ship rolled and heaved. All the while, a couple of bold seamen, swaying fearlessly in the gale, were working on the tangled topsail as the ship pitched in the towering swell.

Finally, the job was done and the men shinned down to the deck. Mungo was surprised that one was the young man, Adam Goss, who'd given his trade as carpenter. Well, if chippies could climb the rigging in a storm, so could gunners! But he wasn't going to go blabbing to Captain Kidd.

For the rest of the night it was all hands on deck as the brig rode out the storm. Mungo played his part, hauling hundreds of yards of hemp rope on pulleys until his hands were raw and bleeding. In turn, he was sent up the rigging to secure the mainstays of the mast and the ratlines running across.

What astonished Mungo when he took a breather was that, despite the heaving ship, he wasn't seasick – and on his maiden voyage too. He'd had no time to give it a thought. Perhaps that was the secret.

In all the night's work he hadn't once caught a glimpse of Gunner Blood and his companion. Perhaps they were still skulking down below. Or maybe they were bending over buckets, giving the stew a second visit.

But 'Hawkeye' Kidd missed nothing on board his ship. Next morning, as the ship sailed on a smooth iron-grey sea, he summoned his cabin boy.

Kidd was sitting at his desk like a judge in wig and gown, passing sentence.

'Master Mullins, ye did tolerably well last night – for such a wee fellow. Better than some twice your size. I want you to know I'm satisfied.'

Abruptly his manner changed, and the slight smile left his lips.

'Not all my crew pulled their weight. I'll not have slackers on this ship. Yon Gunner Blood and his mate need talking to. Send them to me before ye turn in.'

Once again the Captain was fashioning a rod for Mungo's back. The last thing he needed was to provoke Blood and Weasel into an early move.

Reluctantly, he made his way below to pass on

the command. He found the two slackers asleep where he'd left them the night before. His words had no effect, drowned out by snores. Obviously, they were sleeping off the rum.

There was nothing for it but to shake Blood by the shoulder. This he did several times until the man stirred and opened one bloodshot eye. He looked and sounded like a bear with a sore head.

'Wassup? Geroff!'

'Captain says to report to him at once,' Mungo said, taking a step back.

It took a while for Blood to take in what he'd said. Then, with a stream of curses, he swung a boot. Mungo dodged the blow.

'Why, you little runt,' he shouted. 'You know what we do to nasty vermin who tell tales on their shipmates – cook finds their head stuffed in a pot of boiling water; or they get chopped up for stew.'

It was no use explaining that the Captain's keen eye missed nothing. Mungo had kept his mouth shut. He wasn't a tale-tit. He turned and headed for the galley.

Whatever punishment Kidd meted out, Blood and Weasel skulked about the ship, looking daggers at the officers and kicking anything that got in their way. Mungo did his best to give them a wide berth. But inevitably their paths crossed now and then. And if looks could kill, the cabin boy knew he'd be fish food on the ocean bed.

Thirty-one

As soon as he could, Bibby sailed into a sheltered bay and dropped anchor. He needed to give the slaves fresh air, water and nourishment before more died on him and cut his profits. It was late morning when his human cargo was ferried ashore to the small island.

Like other slaves, Abena found it hard at first to stand steady; the ground seemed to be moving beneath her like the sea, making her giddy. It took several minutes for her to stand upright and take faltering steps over the soft sand.

Once she'd grown her new land legs, she gazed about in surprise. The warmth of the sun on her back, the white sand beneath her feet, the coconut palms along the fringes of the shore, even the birds and butterflies reminded her of home. Breezes in the palm trees murmured 'Africa'; birds called to her in the language of her homeland. At any moment she expected to see a wild pig or rabbit, even an elephant, poke its nose or trunk through the bush.

Had she come full circle and landed on the African coast? Or was the world just like her village, with straw-roofed huts and waving palm trees?

Wherever she was, one stark fact remained: she and

the others were slaves, the property of the Red Faces to do what they liked with.

Once off the ship, the crew was acting in a strange manner. For a start, they were removing the men's ankle chains. How odd. On board ship the men had been kept shackled when there was nowhere to run to; yet here on the island they were free to run where they wanted – at least, those who were in a fit state to run anywhere.

The island was small, surrounded by the open sea; the only path of escape was the tossing waves that crashed on to the sandy shore. Yet Red Faces guarded the long-boats with muskets.

Most of the men were in a pitiful state, no more than walking skeletons, their ribcages pushing through skin drawn tightly over their bodies, their arms and legs mere skinny sticks, their faces expressionless skulls. Even without shackles, most lay prostrate on the sand in the same posture as on the ship, as if their bodies were bent into one position.

That didn't suit the sailors. They hadn't brought them here to lie around and die. With whips and clubs they forced the men to their feet and made them hobble about, exercising wasted muscles. All but the lame and dying were marched up and down on the sand like new recruits.

Motioning with their hands, making munching noises and rubbing their stomachs, the sailors gave the slaves to understand that they wanted them to eat and drink to their hearts' content. They didn't have far to look for food, for the island was a veritable larder. Greeny-yellow bananas hung in large bunches from the trees, ripe green figs and brown dates beckoned along the shore, masses of coconuts were just waiting to be knocked down. And there was fruit they'd never seen before.

Abena and the other women were more agile than the men, not having been cooped up in the hold. It didn't take much urging to send them running through the trees, glad to feel the wind in their hair, the grass and moss beneath their feet. As they made the most of their freedom, they stopped to pick fruit and berries, gorging themselves sick on the first food they'd eaten in several days. Here and there they found fresh water in rocky pools and in the folds of large banana leaves.

In the centre of the island, sheltered by trees, they suddenly came upon a large pool. Gleefully, they removed their cloths and jumped in, eager to wash in fresh water for the first time since leaving home. Rubbing themselves down with coconut fibre, they splashed about and swam, uttering cries of joy they hadn't used for a long time. What a relief it was to wash the filth out of their hair, to scrape off the layers of dirt from their bodies!

When they returned to the beach, they brought with them as much fruit as they could carry for the men, many of whom were still lying on the sand where they'd fallen from the long-boat. As they peeled off the fig and banana skins for the men to eat, there was one, his limbs covered in sores and with bones showing through the skin, who screamed abuse at Abena in a language she didn't understand. He knocked the food from her hands, pointing a bony finger towards the Red Faces and making gobbling noises.

'He's afraid of being fattened up for eating,' whispered Afi.

Abena stared at the man in pity.

'Better to be eaten on a full stomach than an empty one,' she said to the man, knowing he wouldn't comprehend.

Brushing past the frightened skeleton, who was still gibbering like a baboon, she dropped her dates and bananas before more grateful invalids who smiled with their eyes, unable to find the strength to speak.

An appetising smell suddenly wafted past their noses. It was meat roasting on a barbecue. Along the beach, sailors had got a bonfire going and were roasting sea turtles they'd caught in the shallows. Unused to human company, the huge beasts had walked innocently into danger and ended up on a spit. So plentiful were they that the Red Faces had started a second fire for the slaves, donating one of their turtles to the feast.

It wasn't long before parties of slaves went turtle

hunting, killing the ungainly creatures with their bare hands. With sharp sticks and stones, they cut off chunks of flesh to roast. The men, who had not eaten fresh meat for several months, eagerly tore off the half-cooked turtle flesh, swallowing it with much smacking of lips, not heeding the almost immediate pain from tender stomachs unaccustomed to such rich fare.

Meanwhile, Abena and the other women did what they could for the weakest, filling gourds with fresh water, and cutting up small pieces of meat for those who couldn't feed themselves.

As dusk was falling, the sailors returned to the ship, leaving the slaves to fend for themselves.

They settled down as best they could to sleep under the stars. The night was warm, the sky cloudless and the sand soft. Those who didn't stretch out on the beach, made sleeping places for themselves in hollows above the sand, not venturing into the trees for fear of snakes and wild animals.

Abena and Afi slept together beside a washed-up tree trunk. How odd it was to listen to long-familiar sounds: bullfrogs croaking from inland pools, bats whirring and twittering in the trees, nocturnal birds – jars, owls, nightingales – cooing and hooting as they went about the hunt. And then there were unwelcome night insects – midges, moths and gnats – who dived upon unguarded flesh.

For the first time in many months Abena was lulled to sleep by the familiar sounds of home, and with a sweet smell in her nostrils.

Thirty-two

In the days to come, Mungo bustled about learning the ropes. Although a few of the crew treated him as a dogsbody, life on board was generally more matey than at the inn. Everyone depended on each other and, as long as they all did their job properly, they got along fine.

Mungo worked hard and was included in the comradeship. That he was a cut above common cabin boys – being able to read and write – endeared him to Captain and crew alike. Another thing: the general respect felt for Mungo made it harder for Weasel and Blood to jump him and seize the sketch. They had to bide their time.

But an air of moody restlessness among the crew mounted as the voyage progressed. Soon the bread was pitted with green mould, the biscuits were crawling with weevils, and the meat and water tasted foul. What was worse, the rum and wine had run out! So when at last they sighted land, the blanket of gloom lifted and the men suddenly came to life.

It was a calm evening as *The Adventure Galley* ploughed through the waves. With a fair wind at their backs they made good headway along the American coast, past Virginia, the Carolinas and Georgia, through the straits between Cuba and Hispaniola, and on to their destination – Jamaica. There they would take on fresh supplies, load up with spices, tobacco and rum, and find their land legs for a few days. At the same time Kidd would take on more crew.

In the fading light, Mungo gazed towards the shore. So this was Jamaica – mysterious isle of African slaves, maybe poor Aba's destination. All he could pick out in the gathering gloom were grey figures crowding about the port below thickly-wooded slopes, rising into hills that blended into the dark purple sky.

The two cooks had told him stories of strange trees bearing large berries and nuts – pineapples, bananas, mangoes and coconuts.

'Watch out, lad, or a great hairy nut will fall on your bonce,' Billy had joked.

'Aye, and don't be mistaking a sleeping crocodile for a log,' added the older man.

Mungo was more fascinated by the people, especially the slaves. He knew what it was like to slave from morn until night at the inn. But at least he was free; he didn't have someone's brand stamped on him. Nor had he been dragged from home to another land, far from family and friends.

Did the slaves have to work like oxen? Or did they run away whenever they could?

What did Africans look like? He'd only seen one,

a young boy. How about girls? Old men and women? Were they black all over? Did they all have brown eyes? Were there ginger-haired Africans?

That night, in his nest beneath the galley table, he couldn't sleep for excitement. Yet an anxious thought kept thrusting itself into his brain. He knew he was safe on board. But ashore would be a different matter. The island was beyond Captain Kidd's protection. So he'd be at the mercy of Blood and Weasel.

Early next morning, as the ship lay at anchor in Port Royal, Mister Mace paid off the crew and gave out Captain's orders:

'We sail in five days. Be back by Thursday noon.'

To cries of 'Aye, aye, Bo'sun,' the men split into parties to haggle over shore prices with the skiffs bobbing alongside.

'Master Mullins!'

It was the bo'sun.

'The Captain wants you to take this letter to the Governor. Look lively, boy!'

Mungo took the long buff envelope, sticking it down the back of his breeches.

'Bring the Governor's reply straight back!' shouted Mister Mace as Mungo climbed the rope ladder into the ship's rowing boat.

'Aye, Aye, Mister Mace,' he called back.

Together with a dozen or so crew he was rowed ashore, clutching his pay for the trip and Mr Jeff's velvet pouch. In his eagerness, he'd forgotten all about the two gunners. Now, as he peered about him, his happy mood suddenly changed. There in the bows sat Blood and Weasel. With an evil grin, the one with the eye-patch drew his right forefinger across his throat.

Mungo had no one to protect him now. Once ashore, should he make a run for it? But where to?

The pair of gunners were first to step ashore, giving each sailor a helping hand from the boat. When it came to Mungo, he felt rough hands grip both his arms and haul him out. Though he called for help, none of the other sailors interfered, thinking the three had a score to settle – as often happened after a long voyage.

'I dunno what you want of me,' Mungo squealed desperately, wriggling like an eel. 'The black slave's dead. The hangman tossed his carcass into the sea.'

Mungo tried a new tack.

'I'm on an errand for Captain Kidd. To Governor Belmont.'

If he thought the names 'Kidd' and 'Belmont' would scare Blood and Weasel into letting him go, he was mistaken. Weasel guffawed loudly and spat a stream of phlegm on to the dusty road.

'That's what we think of Their Nibs!' he said.

If they had no interest in poor Aba, and if they weren't searching for the sketch, then what *were* they after?

Mungo would soon find out.

Thirty-three

They trudged along the quayside for some twenty minutes – time enough to catch the colourful chatter of seamen from all over. Mungo heard the low drawl of Bristol, the nasal mumble of Liverpool, the Cockney slur of London, the harsh accents of Acadia and Newfoundland, and the Yankee twang. Straight from the Middle Passage, with hardly time to draw breath, they were all waiting to take on muscovado sugar, molasses and rum for the return voyage.

Mungo's feet barely touched the ground: his skimpy frame was half-carried, half-dragged along like a sack of cabbages.

He glimpsed passers-by out of the corner of his eye. Most were young black men, weighed down by heavy sacks or bundles of canes; some were driving carts in which white gentlemen sat in black top hats and frock coats, despite the heat.

No black face smiled. None laughed. No one sang. No brown eyes gleamed. No one joked. Their faces had a sullen, helpless look, their eyes a dull glaze, like glass cast up by the sea. They reminded him of mourners at a funeral, grieving deeply for someone or something they had lost. Small wonder. How would he feel if someone had snatched him from his home in a faraway land and brought him in chains across the ocean to slave for white masters?

'Thank God I was born white!' Mungo thought.

But his cuttlefish colour would not save his skin, as he was soon to discover.

Blood and Weasel halted before a ramshackle log cabin set back among the wharves, warehouses and inns. On the door was a sign that he could read, but didn't understand:

VENDUE MASTER

His captors hauled him up the steps to a verandah and shoved open the door.

The room was bare save for some old chests and a makeshift desk cobbled together from two tobacco chests and a wooden plank. There sat a burly, black-bearded fellow flicking beads on a counting frame. He was evidently expecting the visitors for, without a word of greeting, he reached for a brown bottle and poured out three pewter mugs. Mungo's keen nose recognised the sickly-sweet fumes of rum.

'Sit ye down, me hearties,' muttered the Venue Master. 'Come, wet yer whistles on some good Jamaican.'

Blood and Weasel needed no second bidding. They sat on the upturned chests and washed the dust from their tonsils with the fiery brew. After a second and a third mugful, the host noticed Mungo for the first time trying to shrink into the corner shadow.

A low rumble of discontent rose out of the black foliage about his mouth.

'Is that all ye have?'

'Don't judge the bottle by its label,' snapped Blood. 'This 'ere's Kidd's cabin boy, bright as a button and tough as teak. He can handle horses, cook, scrub, clean, skivvy.'

'Yeah, but ee's white. Or are you two colour-blind?! Where's the black slaves you promised?'

'Slipped through our hands,' whined Weasel. 'This kid'll fetch more money. He speaks the lingo, needs no seasoning and he can read and write. So...ee's less cost to keep.'

'But ee's white, in'ee? And white means Christian, not heathen like them nigras. You can't make a silk purse out of a sow's ear, and you can't make a Christian out of a Negro. You know how touchy some masters are about white slaves.'

Blood growled.

'Then sell 'im as a domestic. You can work him 'arder than the natives.'

'Mmmm. That's as may be,' grunted the Master, scratching his beard. 'I bet he's full of lice. Maybe infected with the flux or pox.'

'Who isn't?' said Weasel. 'But he's as fit as a flea,

healthy enough to survive the trip over.'

Turning to Mungo, Blood ordered, 'Strip off, boy, let 'im take a look at yer.'

At first Mungo didn't move, but when Blood raised his fist, he quickly lifted up his shirt and dropped his breeches.

The bearded man shifted his huge bulk over to inspect him for lice, scabs or spots. Mungo was prodded and squeezed, had his ginger hair searched and his teeth examined.

The man wasn't happy.

'Bit pale and skinny, ain't he? Garn, 'ee'll do, I s'pose.'

His eyes suddenly narrowed, spotting the red velvet purse and buff envelope in Mungo's dropped breeches.

'Ay-aye! What 'ave we 'ere?'

He bent down to retrieve the unexpected finds, making the purse tinkle.

'A regular treasure-trove!'

'That's mine,' whined Mungo helplessly.

The man emptied the purse on the plank table and whistled through his black teeth. Blood and Weasel stared angrily at each other, regretting not having frisked their prisoner along the way.

'If cabin boys earn golden guineas, I'm off back to sea!' guffawed the black-bearded man.

'Where'd ya pinch this?' snarled Weasel.

There was no point in lying.

'Mr Jeffs the brewer gave me it – for a rainy day.'

'It's certainly raining now, ain't it, lads? What else 'ave we?'

He picked up the oblong letter, broke the seal and fished out a sheet of paper. Mungo protested.

'I have to deliver that letter to the Governor. It's private.'

'Private? For our dear Governor, eh?'

Taking a flint-stone from his pocket, the man held up the letter by one corner and set light to it. The envelope flared and spluttered, filling the air with smoke.

Mungo took the opportunity to pull up his breeches and let down his shirt, securing the precious sketch under his shirt tail.

''Ow much?'

The question was addressed to Blood and Weasel.

The men haggled for half an hour before agreeing on thirty Jamaican pounds and six bottles of rum. They split the gold guineas three ways before shaking hands on the deal. Blood and Weasel left with their booty, heading straight for a wharfside inn.

Despite Mungo's protestations that he was in the service of the King's Navy and Captain Kidd, it did no good. The Vendue Master clearly had grander plans for him.

'Once you step ashore, laddie, you're beyond Kidd's protection. I've bought you fair and square, so you belong to me. And I know someone who'll pay good money – maybe a hundred guineas – for a white servant who can read and write.'

Mungo soon found himself rattling over a bumpy road in a horse-drawn gig driven by a black slave. He sat opposite the Master, gazing back at the silvery sea with the humpbacked whale of Great Goat Island guarding the approaches to Old Galleon Harbour. They passed lines of pannier mules carrying casks of sugar and rum. Now and then, large wagons of six or more oxen harnessed fore and aft passed by. Mungo soon realised, from the urgent hoots – 'Clear the way or get run down!' – that the strange harnessing was for the steep inclines.

The road led from the coastal plain to jumbled foothills, where the bone-shaking ride worsened as they climbed up steep limestone ridges; the surface here was naked, rain-loosened rock.

As the road levelled out, Mungo looked forlornly at the vast fields of tall straight cane and waving green sugar. He stared at the men, women and children who were weeding, hoeing, digging holes, cutting and tying. It looked back-breaking toil under a merciless sun. Black bodies glistened with sweat, both men and women in nothing more than a breech cloth; some of the women had little ones strapped to their backs as they hacked at the tall cane.

More frightening was the sight of white men on

horseback with knobbed sticks and whips which they frequently brought down on the backs of men and women alike.

Seeing Mungo's fearful glances, the Venue Master growled, 'Thank your lucky stars you've a white hide. Fieldwork's for Negroes – that's what they're born for. Providence has thickened their skins.'

Mungo didn't argue.

They drove along for an hour before turning off the dusty track on to a wide grassy avenue. It led straight as an arrow up a slight incline to a grand country house, square and white with a verandah running round it. All about were flowering trees and bushes of pink, purple and scarlet blooms.

'Orange River Estate,' announced the bearded master. 'See that wooden house? If I strike a bargain with the master, that'll be your new home.'

Mungo gazed towards the mansion. It certainly looked more inviting than Mr Jeff's stables.

Thirty-four

Concern for the slaves' well-being was far from Captain Bibby's mind. The island rest was part of the 'seasoning' of newly-arrived 'Guinea Birds', as the slaves were called. They needed flesh put on their bones. Like the good ship *Sea Venture*, they were also in need of patching up, a lick of tar, a scrub and swab down.

Next morning, the old ship's surgeon, still bleary-eyed from his drunken binge the night before, was rowed ashore. He was to examine each slave for disease – flux dribbling from backsides, or yaws that left large red swellings on the body. For open wounds and ugly sores, the remedy was simple: a bucket of black ointment carried by two sailors. Dipping in a paint brush, the old sawbones dabbed and daubed the worst sores – both to treat the wound and to cover it up with black tar.

For more serious ailments, he turned to the accompanying sailors with a thumbs down sign: that meant they were to set them aside as 'refuse' slaves. Or he did his best to trick buyers into purchasing goods by presenting them as undamaged. Yaws he would disguise with a mixture of iron rust and gunpowder.

Once the medical was over and the medicine applied to those who needed it, the last leg of the voyage could commence. After a week of recuperation on the island, the slaves were ferried back to the brig – all except a few pitiful cases left to die.

There was now an air of relief about the ship: no longer were slaves forbidden to talk, nor did overseers lick their backs with whips or the cat o'nine tails.

As she stood by the rail, Abena was approached by the old African with the broken drum; he asked how she and her family were. She was startled by his knowledge of her language.

'We're fine,' she said. 'I had no idea you spoke Akan.'

'Oh yes, I speak several tongues.'

'So... you knew all along what was being said.'

He smiled a toothless smile.

'You made no sign.'

'Why should I give my own people away? I hate the Red Faces as much as you do.'

She wanted to learn more from the old man.

'Is this your first voyage?'

'No, it's my sixth. The Captain obviously likes my drumming.'

'So you know what awaits us?'

'Yes, you'll be sold to other Red Faces. Most of you will end up working on one of the big plantations – sugar cane or tobacco.'

Abena had no idea what sugar or tobacco were.

'Is it hard work?'

'Back-breaking. But you'll have hundreds of other slaves for company.'

'Will they let my family stay together?'

'Maybe, maybe not. They don't care about families, only about making money.'

With that, he moved away.

All the slaves were lined up on deck for a final seasoning. Once more, the thick black ointment was liberally spread over their sores, and every man and woman was oiled so that their bodies gleamed and glistened in the noonday sunshine. It was like giving a lick of paint to a rusty old kettle full of holes.

For the *Sea Venture*'s Captain the end was in sight. He was about to sell the cargo for whatever price he could squeeze out of the mean plantation owners.

Having dropped anchor in the bay, Captain Bibby searched the sea-line for familiar signs of taverns and warehouses, shacks and bustling crowds. But there was nothing. This was his twentieth and last voyage to Jamaica, yet he'd never landed on this deserted part of the island before.

Since the sea was getting up and dusk was falling, he decided to spend the night onboard; next morning they could either go ashore to investigate and get their bearings, or up anchor and seek out Port Royal – it couldn't be far.

Imagine his amazement when he emerged on deck next morning early to find the ship surrounded by long canoes manned by hostile black men, shaking spears and rusty muskets! Before he could bellow orders, they were swarming all over the ship like locusts ina corn field. There was nothing the weary crew could do.

Had slaves taken over the island and chucked all the whites into the sea?

It didn't dawn on Bibby that he wasn't in the Caribbean. Only when a black man in a scarlet coat and tall top hat came on board did he start to have doubts about his navigation. He stared goggle-eyed at the chief.

'Drunken Lord Willoughby!' he exclaimed. 'How the devil…?'

All at once, the truth fell on his head like a ton of bricks. He was back in Africa!

If Abena's spirits perked up on recognising her native land and people, they were soon dashed on seeing the man who had sold his own people into slavery.

Fortunately for Bibby, he'd kept a stock of rum in his cabin for emergencies – and this could certainly be counted as an emergency. The two chiefs, one red, one black, disappeared into the confines of Bibby's retreat. It was to be several hours before they emerged, both grinning tipsily like a couple of baboons.

In exchange for two brass cannon, twenty cannon balls, ten muskets (without firing pins), buckshot and powder, the *Sea Venture* was restocked with enough food and water to last her six weeks. Lord Willoughby insisted on Bibby waiting for a new coffle of some sixty slaves as part of the bargain.

Within four months of landing back in Africa, the *Sea Venture* finally sailed on the tenth of April 1730, once more Jamaica-bound. The voyage was not as eventful as the first, though the usual average of fifty black bodies was cast into the sea. They encountered no more pirates and made reasonable time, dropping anchor in Port Royal on the first of June – much to Bibby's relief. Henceforth he would carry the tag of 'Bumbling Bibby' for mistaking Africa for the West Indies!

Thirty-five

Not long after arriving, Captain Bibby received his old West Indian agent on board. Over a bottle of rum, they discussed current prices of slaves, sugar, molasses, rum and tobacco.

'I'll be selling off the cargo in the usual fashion.' he told his agent. 'Vendue and scramble. You know the drill: we'll pick out the bruised apples from the barrel and dispose of them by inch of candle.'

'Very well, sir. I know just the tavern, a dark, dingy place where the merchandise won't be exposed to public gaze. The auctioneer's a mate of mine.'

Over the next hour, the two men sorted out the slaves into two lots: prime flesh marked for the scramble and the 'refuse' slaves intended for vendue. They couldn't be too choosy. Strictly speaking, all the slaves were no more than skin and bone, like nags escaped from the knacker's yard. No amount of patching up could disguise the fact that some were on their last legs with the stench and pallor of the grave already on them – those with the flux, yaws, pox, or those who could hardly hobble on disjointed limbs. No one would buy such knackered workhorses.

In the end, some fifty 'refuse' slaves were rowed

ashore along with the Captain and his agent. They made for a nearby tavern with a cheery sign, *The Jolly Sailor*. A large dingy back room had been cleared of tables and benches. To one side, at a desk, sat the auctioneer beside a lighted candle.

The candle provided the only light in the room, its glow reflecting on the faces of a crowd of people standing waiting for the auction to start. The bidding had to be brisk, the custom being to receive bids until an inch of the candle had burned down.

Bibby's factor led in the slaves, one at a time, keeping them in the shadows in one corner of the room. Most of the bidders were poor whites or plantation overseers who hoped to pick up a bargain. Each man had an eye on some slave from whom he'd squeeze enough work to cover the pound or two paid.

Not all the slaves found a buyer; some were obviously too far gone. They were left outside to die on the wharfs without food or water.

Bibby, as was his custom, wet his whistle to celebrate the first batch of sales. Now he waited in the tavern for his Master-at-Arms to ferry over the remaining cargo.

It was early afternoon when strains of the bagpipe announced the arrival of his 'prime' slaves, their bodies glistening with oil. Bibby joined the front of the parade, and they were marched from the docks in a long ragged line through town.

Abena and the other women brought up the rear, the last batch for auction. For the first time she had an opportunity to take stock of this new land. Although blacks were in a majority, it was evidently a white tribal land

The clothing struck her as odd. Despite the midday sun, as hot as in Africa, the Red Faces wore layers of multi-coloured cloth and head coverings. The men had tall black hats and long flowing coats, with leggings and clumsy boots. The women dressed in voluminous, coloured frocks that covered every inch of flesh from neck to toe. All of them were drenched in sweat and constantly fanning themselves.

By contrast, the porters wore nothing but a length of cloth about their loins, as they would in Africa.

At last the parade of slaves reached the public square where a crowd of fifty or sixty men had already gathered, some to purchase, others just to watch and jeer. For Abena it seemed the same process she had witnessed on the sand back in Africa. But there were differences. Whereas the African chief had sold his people for gold, firearms and kettles, now the bargaining was done with pieces of metal exchanged like cowrie shells.

Whole batches of slaves were sold off in lots, with raucous shouts filling the air, competing against one another in shrill or gruff explosions of noise. Each series of bids concluded with the man on the platform banging down his hammer on a wooden box.

So it continued throughout the afternoon, with some men drifting away with their purchases, and others joining the throng. Finally, some seventy slaves – the pick of the cargo – remained. These were disposed of singly, with purchasers scrambling to bid for them at standard prices.

It was already late when the auctioneer came to the dozen women. One by one, Bibby's man led them to the middle of the square, turning them round for all to see. Not everyone had come to purchase; some were clearly there to ogle and manhandle the young women, some pinching and poking grubby fingers into mouths, hair and places that made the women squirm in terror and embarrassment.

Abena, Afi and their mother all huddled together. But they were roughly pulled apart, and first Afi was sold to a crimson-faced man with a large purple nose, then their mother was purchased by a tall man carrying a horse crop.

Only Abena was left unsold. She stood in the square, head bowed, trying to cover her skinny body with her arms. Although the auctioneer shouted several times to the few remaining people, no one seemed interested in the young girl. For a brief moment her hopes rose that she might be taken unsold back to Africa.

But no. All at once she heard a girl's shrill voice

cry out; it was answered by a gruff male voice. They seemed to be bidding against each other. In the end it was the little girl who won. Abena could see her sitting in a gig next to the gruff man, opposite an ugly, red-haired urchin who reminded her of a monkey.

As the hammer-man banged on his box, he pointed from Abena to the little girl, shouting 'Done!'

Meanwhile, mother and sisters hugged and wept on each other's shoulders, knowing they would probably never see each other again. It was Abena who had the last word, as they were led away by their new owners:

'Remember: we *shall* survive!'

Thirty-six

Mungo's gig followed a gravel pathway that meandered round to the back of the house. It was a very warm afternoon, still and peaceful.

All of a sudden, however, the stillness was broken by the sounds of a woman crying, 'No, Massa! No, Massa!' Then the most terrifying shrieks rent the air, sending shivers down Mungo's spine. He had never heard such blood-curdling screams. In between cries he could hear the *swish-sh-sh* of what sounded like a horse whip, whirling through the air before crashing down and biting into flesh; it was like someone mercilessly flogging a horse – save that the cries were unmistakedly human.

As the driver brought the buggy to a halt, the two passengers alighted at the back door.

'Come, lad,' said the Vendue Master, clearly unperturbed. 'Come and see what'll happen if you disobey the master of the house.'

He led Mungo to a clearing at the back of the building where a huddle of servants was gathered. On a bare patch of ground lay a light-brown girl a couple of years older than Mungo. She lay on her belly, arms and legs outstretched and tied to posts. Her bare back and buttocks were both blood raw. Above her stood a tall white man in a blue frock coat and fawn breeches; he was brandishing a whip about ten feet long with a short handle.

The boy watched in horror as the man cracked the whip above his head before bringing it down as hard as he could on the poor girl's back. With each lash she shrieked in pain and writhed like a worm. Every blow tore more skin from her back and made the blood spurt.

To one side, like a boxing referee, stood an overseer, calling out the lashes: '...Twenty-six... twenty-seven... twenty-eight...'

It was too much for the flogger. At 'thirty', he had to stop for a breather, red in the face and perspiring profusely. After a short rest, while a servant brought him a towel and jug of water to quench his thirst, he removed his coat, rolled up his sleeves and took up the whip again. The flogging continued.

On the stroke of thirty-nine, he threw down the whip and nodded to the overseer.

'Rub her raw with pepper and salt, then seal her up!'

With that, he retired to the house.

Mungo screwed his eyes shut. Even on board ship he'd never witnessed flogging so cruel. What on earth had the girl done to warrant such a beating? He asked his companion who, on enquiring, informed Mungo, 'The mulatto house-woman broke a plate.'

'Is that all?'

'Beware, boy! This ain't England and she ain't Christian white. Niggers and mulattos are like wild beasts – whipping's the only language they understand.'

'What's "mulatto"?'

'Gawd! Don't you know nothing?' scoffed the Vendue Master. 'A mulatto's in between, bit of both, bit of tar, bit of apple-blossom. And before you ask, they get that way because white masters do what they please with their female slaves...'

To further piteous screams as pepper and salt were rubbed into the bleeding wounds, Mungo had to watch the last stage of the punishment. The overseer heated up a large red sealing stick and dropped the molten wax into each raw strip of exposed flesh. The pain must have been excruciating. Fortunately, the girl fainted away and lay still and lifeless.

'Methinks the Master'll need a new slave. Come, boy.' Taking Mungo by the arm, the burly man led the boy through the latch-gate of a long, white, sharp-pointed fence, down a path that bisected a neat flower garden, to the back entrance of the house. An old black man with no ears stood barring the doorway.

'Old Bones, go tell Mr Trelawny that Mr Lee, the Vendue Master, has something for him.'

Old Bones shuffled away down a narrow corridor.

As Mungo stood on the porch, he felt the hot sun

on his back, smelt the sickly-sweet fragrance of sugar hanging in the air and caught the tinkling of a spinet coming from somewhere inside the house. Through the open door he glimpsed dusky women going about their chores – washing, cooking, mangling, scrubbing, peeling.

The baking sun, the sickly smell, the tinny spinet and the kitchen chores all contrasted shockingly with the screams, smells and sights of the flogging. Was life so cheap you could whip someone to death for breaking a plate?

The old manservant reminded Mungo of Mr Jeff's clip-clop parlour maid; unlike snooty Molly, however, Old Bones showed no sign of airs and graces. Mungo wondered whether his ears had been cut off as punishment for some minor misdemeanour.

He hardly heard the footsteps returning over the kitchen flagstones. The black man didn't speak, he just gestured for them to go round to the front. Mungo noticed that he was missing several fingers.

With the boy in tow, Mr Lee marched quickly to the front façade where the same tall man in blue frock coat and fawn breeches was lounging back in a rocking chair on the verandah. He was evidently recovering from his strenuous exertions, for he had a large jug of rum punch at his elbow. A little girl in red slippers, frilly white pantaloons and a pink lacy frock was playing with a frisky spaniel, bundles of gold ringlets bouncing on her thin shoulders.

Catching sight of the two whites approaching, the plantation owner spoke sharply to the girl and she ran off towards a paddock of grey and chestnut horses, with the dog frolicking along beside her.

'Good morrow, Mr Trelawny,' called the Vendue Master. 'A fine example you show, sir.'

Mr Trelawny was in his early thirties, with a shock of fair hair overhanging a pale brow that contrasted oddly with a thin red nose, bloodshot eyes, ruddy cheeks and a purple neck. His neatly-clipped moustache marked him out as a military man, but his unhealthy pallor and pot-belly indicated someone fast going to seed.

Mungo had seen such types back at the inn. Evidently Mr Trelawny partook too much of the fruit of his sugar harvest.

'Good day to you, Mr Lee. Aye, the whip is all those apes understand. They need a regular licking to bring them to heel.'

'Good for you, sir.'

'Now, what can I do for you?'

Mr Lee smiled broadly. 'It's more what I can do for you, sir.' He winked, pointing to the boy.

'I offer you one white slave, house-trained, very willing, speaks English – can even read and write. A rarity in these parts.'

The plantation owner tossed a full glass of punch down his gullet – offering none to the guests. All the while he was peering at Mungo. From the expression on his face he obviously didn't like what he saw.

'Why would I need a white domestic? If he runs away, there's no telling him from free whites, like salt in a sugar bowl. And he's likely to be uppity, hard to break with the whip.'

'But, sir, think of the money he'll save you – an indentured servant for five-to-ten years, no worry about health or providing for old age – unlike them blacks. You can work 'im 'arder. And… if he pegs out, too bad. Bob's yer uncle, Fanny's yer aunt!'

Mr Trelawny snorted.

'By the look of his carrot top, he's damn Irish or Scots – and you know what trouble they cause, worse than crocodiles.'

'He's as English as the King! Speak up, lad.'

'English,' confirmed Mungo, wondering what he was letting himself in for.

'He can curry a horse, feed animals, wash and serve without breaking any plates, scrub floors, do any household chore…'

The plantation owner rubbed his chin.

'I don't know. He looks too smart-arsed to me.'

Mr Lee tried one last ploy.

'He could amuse your dear little girl; he speaks the lingo. He could read to her, play games, teach her to ride, get her from under your feet.'

That obviously struck a chord. Mr Trelawny

stopped rocking and stared hard.

'How much are you asking?'

'Well, now... Since I'm selling him as a bonded servant, not a lifetime slave, I reckon 'ee's worth a couple of hundred. But, sir, as you're a Christian gentleman, he's yorn for one-fifty.'

For the second time that day, Mungo discovered how much he was worth. By the time he'd been knocked down for a hundred pounds, he'd become a domestic, a bonded servant on Mr Trelawny's sugar plantation.

At least his throat hadn't been cut, his flesh wasn't feeding the sharks, and his body wasn't being flayed. Not for the moment, anyway...

Thirty-seven

At the ringing of a hand-bell, a female servant appeared. She stood quietly, hands behind her back, awaiting orders. Mr Trelawny seemed to have dozed off, either from his flogging exertions or from the rum. The servant and boy stood staring at each other, not knowing whether to speak.

The young woman wasn't black and she wasn't white; she was in between. Under her kerchief her hair wasn't tight black curls or light wavy tresses; it was a sort of rusty frizzle, like a bramble bush, swept up in a discoloured band tied in a knot. She was wearing a plain grey smock down to her ankles, with bare feet.

Eventually the Master's eyes opened and, seeing the two blurred figures, he waved a hand dismissively, grunting, 'Take him away, Molly.' Then his head dropped back on his chest and he started snoring.

Mungo was eager to ask questions, but Molly put a finger to her lips and gave him a hard stare. Only when they reached the kitchen did she open her mouth.

'Speak only when spoken to. 'Cept in the kitchen!'

At Mungo's puzzled frown, she gave him a toothy grin.

'How did a ginger tom like you end up here?'

Mungo told his story briefly to an audience of six wide-eyed women.

'Oh, so Daddy wants you to look after his little girl, does he? He certainly can't manage on his own.'

'Where's her mother?' asked Mungo.

'Down the garden.'

Mungo peered through the steamed-up window, searching for the mistress.

'Six feet under, feeding the worms,' muttered an older woman, peeling yams.

'Good riddance too,' grunted another.

'Fever,' added Molly. 'Pink ladies aren't made for dark tropics.'

'They melt like butter on the hob,' added a light-skinned young woman.

'Now then, Master Mungo,' said Molly, 'let's do the introductions before the Master comes a'prowling. This 'ere's Mulatto Mary, seamstress and chambermaid. Creole Sue – our washerwoman. Mulatto Nelly – cook. Congo Nancy and Judy are water carriers. You've met Old Bones who runs – or should I say hobbles – errands and drives the gig...'

She hesitated.

'We're one missing at the moment – poor Phibia...'

Her voice tailed off.

All the house-women were different shades of brown, like a sack of walnuts, thought Mungo. Only Old Bones was black, as black as night. Judging from her leathery paleness, Creole seemed to mean that Sue's parents must have been white before the Jamaican sun got at them.

'What do you do?' the boy asked Molly.

'Me, I'm just plain old Mulatto Molly, house woman, working my fingers to the bone at the Master's beck and call. Take him his rum and 'baccy, wash him in his bath tub – that's worse than all the licks imaginable – dress him, serve him his meals, dance to his spoiled daughter's tune, make sure she does her music practice, keep her clean. What else? I learned some doctoring from my mother: so I'll put herbs and healing spells on poor Phibia now the overseer's done with her. God knows if it'll help.'

Mungo would like to have asked more. But he saw such an odd look in Mulatto Molly's eyes that he thought it best to change the subject.

'Where do I doss down?'

'We each have our own little hut beyond the fence. Until the Master decides, you'd better shack up with Old Bones.'

The earless old African in canvas jacket, breeches and sandals made no sign he understood.

'In the meantime, muck in with us.'

Mungo sat on a three-legged stool next to Mulatto Nelly and began peeling sweet potatoes, cabbages and plantains. The rest of the day passed uneventfully. He ate his fill, swept the clearing clean of Phibia's blood and skin, washed in the nearby stream and waited to be summoned.

No call came. The Master was dead to the world in a drunken sleep.

Late that evening, Old Bones made a gesture for him to follow. Together, the old man and boy walked down a path towards a row of wooden huts spaced higgledy-piggledy in a semi-circle. For the first time in his life, Mungo heard the strange night sounds of a tropical land: cicadas ticking, crickets clicking, lizards rustling in the bushes, the whirring of night birds, the barking of distant dogs. And there was something else, odd and exciting: somewhere in the distance, drums were beating a pulsating rhythm.

He wondered whether the drumbeat was Africans talking to each other in their own language, to their families scattered about the island.

At the very end of the row, the old African entered a dark, oblong hovel with thatched roof, much smaller than Mr Jeff's stable. Yet the smell was not so different: fresh straw, rain-soaked timbers drying in the night air, and Mother Earth – homely, comforting, sweet-smelling.

In one corner was a straw palliasse. There was no furniture. Beside the entrance were an earthenware pot and a calabash of water. A shaft of moonlight came from a small open space above.

So far the African hadn't uttered a word. Perhaps his

tongue had been cut off along with his ears and fingers? But now he knelt down and touched his forehead to the hard mud-packed floor and spoke softly in a secret tongue. All the while, he twirled a pair of cock feathers between two fingers.

Mungo remembered similar prayers at a service in the Garrison Church – he'd earned a few groats from scrubbing the flagstones clean, the chaplain being one of Mr Feltham's best customers. The faithful had also knelt and bowed their heads, mumbling spells and prayers. He didn't remember any cock feathers, though.

When Old Bones had finished, he sat bolt upright and said in a low rumbling voice, 'Take the bed.'

Mungo jumped as if he'd been stung.

'So you speak English, Mr Bones?'

The man sighed deeply before replying.

'My name is Kwasi.'

He spoke so proudly Mungo apologised at once.

'Sorry, Mr Kwasi, I didn't know.'

'What is your name?'

'Mungo. Mungo Mullins.'

'Your real name?'

'Yes, that is my real name. My father was Mullins. He called me Mungo.'

Now they were talking, Mungo took the opportunity to learn more about slave life. And he found Kwasi a ready talker; he seemed to trust the red-haired boy.

'Where were you born?' asked Mungo.

'Far away,' came the reply. 'Across the sea. Ashanti lands. Africa.'

'Were you taken prisoner?'

He nodded, adding, 'Sold, branded, transported, made a slave.'

'Didn't you ever try to escape?'

The old African remained silent.

Surely slaves put up a struggle? thought Mungo. They were many, their masters few. Didn't they fight back? But then Mungo realised: where would they go? They could hardly run away to Africa!

A low rumble issued from the old man.

'Oh, yes-s-s. Ever since the Spanish and English brought us here, there have been revolts. Sometimes ones and twos, sometimes a dozen or more, sometimes whole bands have burned down estates and "pulled foot", as they call running away.'

'Where do they go?'

Kwasi put a finger to his lips, stood up and beckoned the boy to follow. Outside the hut he pointed towards the dark sky. At first Mungo thought he meant his spirit had escaped to some heavenly home. But then, in the moonlight, Mungo saw the dim outline of mountains wreathed in misty clouds.

'To the Blue Mountains, home of runaway slaves, hundreds of them. Entire villages are free from white whips.'

'What happened to you?'

Kwasi said nothing. He just shrugged and held up his hands to show his missing fingers. Then he covered his ear-hole scars. Lastly, he removed his sandals.

Mungo gasped. Half of both feet were missing! No wonder the old man limped, with just toeless stumps for feet.

'So you were caught...'

Yes. But... one day, one day soon, we'll overthrow the cruel masters and break free.' He sighed deeply.

'Not in my lifetime, I fear.'

There was nothing more to say. The old African pulled a mat from under the lumpy palliasse and lay down in the opposite corner. Judging from his heavy, even breathing he was soon fast asleep.

Mungo sat on the straw bed, clutching his knees to his chest, trying to take in all the day's impressions: the brutal flogging of the girl still made his flesh creep, giving him a feeling of utter helplessness. He was a slave-servant, defenceless. What could he do?

By day the overseers kept close watch, by night savage guard dogs roamed the estate. So there was no escaping.

Yet Kwasi hadn't given in. He had kept his own name, deep down inside him, where they couldn't reach, where no one could touch him. He was Kwasi. Not a humiliating name like Old Bones or Mullato

Molly or Creole Sue or Congo Nancy. He hadn't surrendered his spirit. He had run away three times, judging by his chopped-off fingers, ears and toes... Now, he couldn't hobble anywhere beyond the estate.

But the white slave masters had not broken Kwasi's spirit.

And they won't break mine! vowed Mungo.

Thirty-eight

Next morning, even before the sky had rubbed the sleepy dust from its eyes, Mungo woke to an eerie sound. It seemed to roll in from the sea, like a siren wailing. It echoed across the valley and bounced back off the thickly-wooded hills. The boy sat up with a start. On board ship he'd heard terrifying tales of an earthquake sending half of Port Royal into the sea some years back. But the ground beneath him was as firm as a rock.

A low growl issued from the far corner.

'The conch shell.'

Mungo knew about cockles and mussels – but not about a shell large enough to be heard over an entire island.

'Wake-up call,' muttered Kwasi, hauling himself up. 'Time for slaves to work under the whip. In crop time, that means well before sun-up to way past sun-down.'

'Every day?'

'December to May, yes. That's harvest time. The rest of the year, no. Our masters are god-fearing Christians. Sundays are for church.'

'Do we *all* have to go to church?'

Old Kwasi laughed bitterly, like leaves crackling underfoot.

'Church isn't for black folk,' he said. 'We've no souls to save. So we work on our plots of land; that saves the Master having to feed us.'

'Do I have a soul?' asked Mungo.

The old African looked him up and down, as if searching for a sign.

'I guess so. Souls are white, like foam on waves. You can't see them, but you whiteys have to keep polishing them, saying your prayers and going to church regularly.'

He gave a throaty chuckle. 'It's just as well we don't have souls; saves us all that soul-scrubbing. Now, Master Mungo, time to greet the day.'

Mungo followed the old man as he hobbled from the hut, down through the trees, to a fast-flowing stream.

'Watch out for snakes!'

With a shiver, Mungo glanced around as Kwasi splashed naked in the reeds, hidden from the women bathing farther along. The boy followed suit, stripping off and plunging into the cold tumbling stream. They dried themselves on grass and rushes before pulling on their clothes and moving off towards the big house.

'Funny the colours that gods gave man,' said Kwasi. 'We bathe more often than whites, yet we're still black and you're still white.'

He chuckled to himself.

The washerwoman Creole Sue called hello to him from the stream as she beat sheets and clothes upon some rocks; and the kitchen women greeted them as 'Old Bones' and 'Master Mungo'. They were already busy at their tasks.

The two water-carriers were trotting back and forth to the stream, filling up wooden pails ready to take to the fields.

It was some time before Mulatto Molly appeared. Not only had she fed some gruel to the feverish Phibia, she'd already milked eleven cows in the meadow before sunrise. Now Mungo caught a glimpse of her staggering towards the buttery, pushing a hand-cart carrying four milk churns.

He ran out into the yard, opened the buttery door and helped lift the heavy milk churns from the cart. He was used to bulky beer barrels and crates, yet the churns made him stagger.

Once the cart was empty, Molly said, 'Grab a spatula and separate off the dead gnats and cream while I churn the butter.'

In a low voice, she added, 'And take the dipper and help yourself to some creamy cow juice. You need building up; you're nothing but skin and bone.'

Mungo mumbled his thanks and asked after the sick girl.

'Say a prayer,' was all Molly said.

It wasn't until mid-morning that the Master sent for his new servant. Mr Trelawny wasn't in the best of moods.

'God knows why I wasted good money on a thieving Irish brat like you. You'll probably poison us all.'

Mungo didn't waste his breath on a reply.

Mr Trelawny ranted on for several minutes, but he was interrupted by squeals and whoops coming down the stairs. At once his tone changed abruptly to that of a simpering father.

'Daddy!' squealed the girl Mungo had glimpsed the day before; she was still in her frilly nightcap and gown. She ran to her father, threw two pink chubby arms about his neck and kissed him on both cheeks.

He was sitting at a mahogany desk in the large living room. Curtains of blue and white dimity filtered the bright sunshine. A clock ticked loudly on the walnut mantelpiece, and two looking-glasses hung on opposite walls; half-reflected in them were a couple of paintings of a serious-looking woman. Behind the desk was a glass case holding two silver-mounted pistols, six guns, two hilted swords and a cane – no doubt to ward off attack from crazed slaves.

'Hetty, honeybun,' he exclaimed, disentangling himself from her embrace and pointing to Mungo. 'I've a present for you.'

The little girl turned her gaze on the ginger-haired

urchin standing by the door. Right away the sweet baby face and childish cooing gave way to an ugly scowl and pig-like snorts.

'Not that thing!' she flung at Mungo.

'"That thing" is going to teach you to read and write,' her father said.

'I don't want him. He's horrid!'

'Now, now, sweety-pie, you can't always have your own way. As it is, you've driven three nannies away. This boy's your personal servant. With Mummy gone and the plantation to attend to, I simply don't have time to run after you.'

At the words 'personal servant', she hesitated.

'To do what I like with?'

'We-e-ell, yes. But you've got to learn as well.'

She considered the situation.

'A horsey to ride and whip around the paddock? Gee-up, Neddy!'

Going up to Mungo, she shouted at him, 'Can you tell stories, boy?'

Mungo decided it was time to put his foot down, even if he did earn a beating for his cheek.

'I'm not a horse. I'm a human being. I won't be whipped. But, yes, I can tell stories and sing the nursery rhymes my mother taught me.'

'Tell me a nursery rhyme,' she cried.

'Say "please",' Mungo insisted.

Mr Trelawny let his daughter reply. She yelled at

this insolent boy, 'You'll do as I say! You're my servant. I'll have you flogged.'

'No "please", no story,' Mungo said calmly.

She stamped her foot and stormed off in tears of rage, but a few minutes later she was back, muttering in a tiny voice, 'I want a story.'

Mungo remained tight-lipped.

'Please...'

For the next hour, Mungo went through his repertoire of songs and nursery rhymes: *Ring a ring o'roses* and *Here we go round the mulberry bush* were both well received.

When her father returned from inspecting the household, he found his daughter sitting at the spinet practising her scales – to Mungo's promise of stories of *The Three Bears* and *Little Red Riding Hood*, once her practice was over.

Mr Trelawny smiled to himself.

'Well – there's a hundred pounds well spent!'

Thirty-nine

Not every day passed as smoothly as the first. Young Hetty was as changeable as the weather: warm and sunny one minute, cold and stormy the next. There were times when no threat or promise could cure her; even her father made himself scarce until the hurricane had blown itself out.

About two weeks after Mungo had begun his nanny duties, Phibia died. If he felt a twinge of conscience for Phibia's death, Mr Trelawny didn't show it. With female slaves two a penny, he thought nothing of flogging one to death and replacing her with another. Show who's boss and hang the consequences! – that was his motto.

'How'd you like a ride to town, sweetie?' he asked Hetty one day. 'You can help Daddy choose a new woman.'

'Can Mungo come too?' she whined.

The Master looked surprised.

'If he must. He can sit up front.'

So it was that the four of them rode to market. Mungo sat on the driver's seat next to the old African. Once more he stared in awe at the passing sugar fields – not to admire the tall swaying crop that earned

Mr Trelawny his fortune, but to stare wonderingly at the slaves – hundreds and hundreds of them – bending low as they cut the thick cane with machetes, tied them up in bundles and hauled them off to the factory.

All the while, men on horseback snaked out cow-hide whips on to naked backs. There seemed no reason for the whip other than to keep the slaves in constant fear and amuse the sadistic overseer. What struck Mungo was the sullen silence that hung above the fields, like a brooding storm cloud about to burst.

As they left the plantation behind and drove into town, Mr Trelawny suddenly gave a shout,

'Who – o – ahh!'

When the driver hauled on the reins, bringing the gig to a standstill, Mr Trelawny stepped on to the road, lifting out his daughter behind him; he beckoned Mungo to follow.

At the end of the street stood a small crowd of gentlemen in their Sunday best, their shiny stove-pipe hats shielding them from the sun, their eyes fixed intently on stock being auctioned off in the square ahead of them.

'What am I bid, gentlemen, for this fine buck?' boomed a fog-horn voice. 'Short neck, firm limbs, fine back, good breeding stock. Strong as an ox and well seasoned. A hundred?'

At first Mungo thought it was a cattle market. But as he came closer, he saw the stock for sale was not animals, but human beings. Black beings. This was his first sight of a slave auction. The poor men were mostly scared out of their wits, as if they were being sold for slaughter, like cattle. But a few stood staring defiantly at their prospective masters. The slaves were naked save for flimsy loincloths, their skins glistening with oil and sweat.

Mr Trelawny waited patiently, exchanging pleasantries with his neighbours. Little Hetty, meanwhile, was fascinated by these naked chocolate soldiers and giggled at their ungainly gait as they shuffled along in leg shackles.

Having sold off the men, the auctioneer at last came to the female slaves. There were twelve; three appeared to be from the same family by the way they huddled together – a mother and two daughters, the younger about Mungo's age.

One by one, the auctioneer led them to the middle of the square, turning them slowly round for all to see. Like the men, they were naked apart from a 'shame-cloth'.

'See for yourselves, gentlemen – prime flesh, born to toil, good child-bearing hips.'

A few men stepped forward, prodding the women as a farmer would a calf or lamb he was about to purchase – squeezing arms and thighs and searching heads for lice.

Mr Trelawny shook his head, shouting to the

auctioneer, 'No mulattos, Sykes?'

'Not today, Mr Trelawny. This lot's Guinea Birds, fresh ashore.'

Just then the youngest of the little family was led out. Despite obvious attempts to cover up sores and lashes with black ointment, her front and back were criss-crossed with livid crimson patches that stood out like crawling caterpillars. She was a tall, bony creature, stooping, head bowed, hands cupped before her as if trying to cover her small breasts.

'Fine mare,' shouted the auctioneer. 'Slender make, large eye (he forced her head up with a riding crop), prominent forehead and straight nose, good curly head of hair... Can tell the hour by the clock.'

Although bidding started at no more than a few pounds, no one took up the offer.

Uninterested, Mungo's master turned away. But Hetty pulled at his sleeve.

'I want her, Daddy!' she trilled, jumping up and down in excitement. 'Go on, buy her for me.'

'I don't need a black woman!' he snorted in disgust. 'Even if she can tell the time!'

His daughter wouldn't let go.

'Oh, go on, Daddy, darling Daddy. She can look after the garden and orchard, now that Mummy and Phibia aren't here.'

'No, no, too many black girls spell trouble: they're lying, idle, lazy, thieving bitches.'

Hetty almost always got her way, and she did so now. The young black girl was knocked down for seven pounds – cheap because of her age.

'Sold to Mr Trelawny of Orange River Estate!' yelled the auctioneer, banging his hammer down on a wooden box.

Abena, her mother and Afi hugged and cried on each other's shoulders. Each went their separate ways; Abena was led to the waiting gig and forced to sit up front between Mungo and the driver – so that she couldn't throw herself beneath the wheels.

Forty

Wedged between the African driver and the little red monkey, Abena was carted off. Her only consolation was that scary tales of being eaten by white cannibals were disproved by the masses of black people about. True, they were obviously slaves of the big white chiefs – like the man holding the reins beside her, though she did notice that someone had eaten his ears and some of his fingers. Perhaps they'd eaten his tongue too, for he only grunted and moo-moo'd to the two ponies pulling the cart.

Behind her, the little pink girl chattered and squealed as if being taken out for a birthday treat. Abena recognised a few words: 'Yess-ss.' 'No-o-o.' 'Hey-y-y, you-ou!' – the last addressed to the flame-haired boy whose bony elbows were digging into her ribs. He seemed to speak the Red Man's language too, for he answered back in their tongue: 'Yess-ss, Meess-ss... Yessir! Yessir!'

Was he the man's son, brother of the little girl? It never entered her head that he was a white slave.

Everything was so new, it was hard to take it all in. The tipsy sailors staggering into the road from noisy houses with swinging signs reminded her of the medicine man who'd been the cause of her misery. If it weren't for his black skin, he'd be at home here with the shouting, singing, rum-swigging crew.

So many tall huts, one on top of the other, all built of wood, with walls you could see through, and all painted in different colours – red and orange, green and white, yellow and black. Some had doors of one colour, walls of another and roofs of yet another, with little yellow hats on top.

What a contrast in the people! There weren't like the villagers at home or the sailors on board ship. Some looked so poor, they stumbled along carrying half an elephant-load on their backs, wearing nothing but a skimpy loincloth, oblivious to their own nakedness – women as well as men.

Yet grand white chieftains in their royal finery, carrying nothing at all, trundled by in horse-drawn carts. So many kings and queens for such a small land! And there were odd, light-dark-skinned men who rode along the road on mules, shouting down to the blacks, but up to the whites.

She closed her eyes, lulled by the rocking of the cart.

When she awoke, she was alarmed to find her head resting on the red boy's shoulder. The cart had halted at the back of a grand palace as big as a whole village with rows of wooden huts scattered all about.

Hardly had she had time to look around than a light-dark-skinned woman emerged from the house and, after a brief exchange with the white chief, led Abena up a slope to a small shack containing nothing but a mattress that smelled of damp hay. Evidently, this was to be her lodging. What a luxury after the stinking, bucking ship!

She had no idea what the woman was saying. Her voice didn't contain the harsh tone of the masters, nor did it whimper or cringe. One word the grey-brown woman kept repeating was, 'Peggy… Peggy.'

Abena had no idea what it meant. The woman clearly wanted her to speak it, so she tried: 'Pay-gee, Pay-gee…' No, she didn't like the sound of it at all. But the woman was patient, prodding her own chest and saying, 'Moll-ee… Moll-ee,' then pointing to Abena and saying, 'Peggy'.

Finally, the girl caught on. For some reason, they must think her name was 'Peggy.' She shook her head firmly, repeating over and over: 'Abena. Abena. Abena!'

Either Molly was deaf, or she was insisting on Abena having a new name in this new land.

No! Abena wasn't having that. Abena was her name, the one her mother and sister knew her by. No, no, no! They could beat her, starve her, put their brand on her. But they couldn't take away her name. Never!

It was Abena who had the last word. As Molly walked away from the hut, shouts of 'Abena' followed her all the way back to the big house. Next time Molly came to see her, later that day, it was to bring food –

a pot of boiled yams and plantains with salted pork. This time, however, Molly avoided mention of her slave name. With a sigh, she thought to herself, 'Poor girl, she'll have to learn the hard way. First they'll break her spirit, then, if she doesn't obey, they'll break her bones. She needs more seasoning. Some Guinea Birds are like that – you have to break them in two and start anew.'

The next few days were spent on the seasoning: Abena was left to wander about the plantation, getting her bearings, seeing how field slaves toiled from dawn to dusk. She watched in fascination as they swung their machetes against the base of the tall cane; she saw the green leaves tremble as the cane toppled and fell upon the gritty, hard-baked earth. It was obviously back-breaking toil under a hot midday sun. With all that stooping and chopping, no wonder their hands were blistered and bleeding as they tossed bundles of cane into mule carts.

Abena wondered if this was the work her mother and Afi had to do. How long would her mother last? She wasn't strong and, with her bad back, she'd be unable to toil as a field slave more than a few weeks.

'Mama, Mama,' she cried to herself, seeing older women staggering under large bundles of cane. 'I'll come to save you. I will!'

If only she knew where her mother was.

Later that day, she followed the slaves back to their

huts and noticed that they often had their own patch of earth to grow yam and maize, sorrel and nutmeg – to sell at market or feed themselves, she couldn't tell.

She saw that on Saturday evenings they gathered under a big ceida tree to play music from the 'old country', and to sing and dance. From the edge of the circle Abena watched as the drumming began – knuckles on tin plates or a calabash or a stew pot, or a stick on a tree or stick on stick… Gradually, the rhythm captured hands and feet so that feet started to twitch, heels began to pound the hard earth, until everyone was dancing.

Then, all at once, dead on nine o'clock, a gong sounded, the drumming and dancing stopped, and the crowd dispersed to their huts. The curfew gong drove everyone back to their huts. Woe betide anyone caught out after dark.

Sunday was a free day, and Abena was surprised to see slaves leave the plantation and line the route leading to town. Some spread out bananas on the grass verge, others plantains, cassava, yams, bundles of grass, even chickens. Passing mule carts would pull up, and drivers and vendors would haggle over prices in some strange tongue before exchanging wares for metal coins.

She tried to talk to some women, but either they didn't speak her language or they were too frightened, shaking their heads and ignoring her.

As she was returning from the Sunday market, Abena saw Molly waiting for her with a smiling black woman.

'How are you, girl?' the woman asked in a sing-song Ashanti accent.

Abena kept sullenly silent.

'Where you from?'

More silence.

Molly left them to it, and the woman tried again.

'You speak Ashanti?'

This time Abena nodded.

'My name is Ama, though I'm known by my slave name – Annie.'

Abena gave her a hard stare before saying abruptly, 'I'll never take a slave name.'

'Yes, yes, that's what we all say. But it's best to answer to "Peggy" when the Master calls, or you'll be in trouble. It only means "girl" or "woman", nothing more. The masters are so stupid they can't say our names, only their own.'

'What do you do?' asked Abena warily. 'Cut cane?'

'No, I work in the sugar factory.'

'Will I go there?'

'No, I'm to take you to your mistress. The Master's daughter wants you as her personal slave."

Abena turned up her nose.

'Slave to a little Red Girl! She can wipe her own bottom.'

'You don't know how lucky you are. Better the caprices of a spoilt girl than the overseer's whip across your back. I'd swap the stifling, stinking factory any day for life at the big house. It's clean and fresh, and full of tasty food. It'll put some flesh on your bones.'

'I won't eat their food!'

Ama gave up. This pig-headed girl needed to learn what being a slave meant.

'I'll come back when you've thought it over,' she said.

Forty-one

Being at the beck and call of the Master's daughter was definitely not to Abena's liking. But the more she thought about it, the more she remembered Ama's words: it was better than slaving in factory or field. During Abena's wanderings, she'd seen women in the sugar fields, bent double, glistening with sweat, sometimes with babies strapped to their backs, and all the while under the overseer's lash if they worked too slowly. Six days a week, sun-up until sun-down.

Was that the fate of her sister and her mother?

When Ama returned next day, Abena had made up her mind.

'All right,' she said. 'When do I start?'

'Master says to season you for a few weeks, give you jobs about the house and yard. He'll summon you when he's good and ready.'

So Abena swept the yard, hoed the garden, churned the butter and did a hundred and one menial chores. She worked sullenly and slowly, unwilling to bend to the white tyrant's will. Every day she received punishment: no food, extra work, beatings. And all this she bore in silence.

One day, Ama came to fetch her.

'The Master reckons you might as well work for his daughter; you're useless at everything else.'

Abena, her head held defiantly, followed the squat older woman along the grassy track to the back of the big house. There they were met by the same old ear-less African who'd driven her in the gig. Without a word, he led the way round the side of the building to the front of the house where, on a white-railed verandah, sat the Master, staring out moodily over his estate.

As the old black man approached, he halted at the foot of the steps, as if not daring to sully the wooden verandah with his dirty sandals.

Waving away the hobbling escort, the Master uttered one word: 'Come.'

Ama took Abena's arm and together they climbed the five spotlessly clean steps to stand in front of Abena's new owner.

Giving the new girl no more than a cursory glance, he barked orders that were translated for her benefit.

'Master says you belong to his daughter; you're hers to do what she wants with. If he hears a single complaint about you, he'll have you roasted on a spit.'

If this pompous brute had spoken Akan, Abena would have told him to his face to go and roast himself. She said as much to Ama. 'Tell him I'll thrash his precious darling's backside if she gives me any cheek.'

'Peggy says she'll do all you say, sir,' said Ama.

Hearing the word 'Peggy', Abena swiftly added, 'And tell the red-faced oaf my name is Abena. Always was, always will be.'

'Peggy says she's very grateful, sir.'

Pointing to the paddock where Hetty could be seen astride the fence, tossing sticks at the horses, the Master shooed the two females away. He raised a glass of rum to his lips, gulped it down and went back to staring into space.

Abena walked alone towards the paddock where the girl in a pink frock was sitting. Hearing her approach, the girl turned round and clapped her hands, shouting, 'Peggy! Peggy! Peggy!'

There followed a tumble of words that went right over Abena's head. All she could tell was that they were spoken in the tone of a little old woman. Abena stood still, spreading her arms wide in incomprehension. That irritated Hetty, and she flung another torrent of words at the puzzled black girl. When Abena did not respond, she jumped down from the fence and raised her horse switch menacingly. She began beating Abena about the legs, making her hop on one foot, trying to dodge the blows. All the while the girl was screaming at the top of her voice – as if blows and shouts would force the slave to understand.

For a few minutes Abena withstood the beating. Then, calmly, she took the switch from the girl's hands and snapped it in two. That done, she released her own flood of words which were just as baffling to the pink girl.

At first, Hetty stood still in astonishment, her mouth gaping. She was not used to being disobeyed, let alone by a slave. Then, all at once, she shrieked at the top of her voice, 'DADDY! DADDY!' and ran back to the house in floods of tears.

Abena knew she was in trouble. Would the Master carry out his threat and roast her on a spit? She wasn't going to stay around to find out. Taking to her heels, she rushed, helter-skelter, anywhere, as long as it was away from the house. The only thought in her mind was to make for the road beyond the estate, where she'd seen women selling their goods.

What was she to do? Stow away on a ship back to Africa? But the very thought of the stinking hold turned her stomach over; she couldn't face that journey again. In any case, her mother and sister were here, somewhere on the island. She made up her mind to go in search of them.

Such a feeling of joy filled her heart as she ran along the mud-beaten track – she couldn't help herself. She shouted at the top of her voice: 'Free! Free!' The words lent wings to her heels and she fairly bounded along. She had no idea where she was going; all she wanted to do was put as many miles as possible between herself and the hated estate. From the brow of a hill, she glimpsed the sea glittering in the distance.

Sea meant harbour; harbour meant *Sea Venture*, the parade and auction in the public square. She had to trace her steps back to the beginning if she was to discover the whereabouts of her mother and sister. Perhaps she would come across someone who spoke her language and could tell her where they were. Maybe she'd see the man with the purple nose...

Distances are deceptive. After an hour she seemed to be getting no closer to the sea; she'd had to slow to a trot, with frequent rests. Her legs and lungs didn't keep pace with the beating of her heart. Every time she heard the rumble of a cart or the clip-clop of hoofs, she dived into bushes until the danger passed. Now, with darkness falling fast, she needed somewhere to rest – somewhere safe, in the open, out of harm's way.

She didn't know whether wild animals roamed the forest – lions or crocodiles. To be on the safe side, she needed to find a sleeping place close to habitation. As luck would have it, she was just approaching an estate; she could see a long row of slave huts. Wild animals might eat her, but humans were also dangerous – they could give her away if they knew she was a runaway.

Abena crept towards the back of the last hut, where the overhanging branches of a leafy tree formed a roof above a hollow between tree and wall. Although the evening was quite chilly, she rolled herself up into a ball like a cat and fell into a fitful sleep, jumping at every rustle and snapping twig about her.

Forty-two

She awoke at dawn with a start. An appetising smell tantalised her nose, reminding her stomach she hadn't eaten since the previous morning. Walking on tip-toe to the corner of the hut, she peered round it. Smoke was drifting up from a fire in front of the hut, and what looked like a chicken leg was roasting.

No one was around. She took a chance. She darted out and snatched up the drumstick before anyone could stop her. In no time at all she was back on the road, chewing the half-cooked meat as she jogged along.

'Sorry,' she mumbled between bites. 'I need strength to be free. You need it only to slave.'

After about a mile she suddenly heard a shout behind her. It made her jump because she hadn't heard the mule cart approach.

'Where ya goin', Missy?'

She ignored the slave talk.

Much to her surprise, the man repeated his question in a language she understood.

'Town,' she said curtly.

'Me too,' the young man said with a broad smile. 'Want a lift?'

'No.'

'Town's miles,' he said, slowing his mules to a trot.

'How many?'

'Oh, about eight or ten.'

She thought it over. It would take hours to walk ten miles. The driver seemed friendly enough and obviously came from her part of Africa.

'All right. Can you drop me off at the main square, where the slave auctions are held?'

'No bother. Jump in.'

She clambered up beside the driver, glad to rest her sore feet.

'Whose slave are you?' he asked.

'I'm *not* a slave.'

Almost as soon as the words jumped out of her mouth, she regretted them. Maybe all blacks were slaves, and she'd given herself away. If she wasn't a slave, she must be *on the run*...

He glanced at her sideways, noticing the branding just inside her thin shirt. But he said nothing and they rode along in silence.

'Whose slave are *you*?' she finally asked.

'Mr Keating's. Manor Farm. I'm fetching provisions from town.'

His answer persuaded her to tell him more.

'I'm looking for my family. We got separated.'

'Recently?'

'About a week ago.'

'So you were sold as slaves?'

There was no point in denying it.

'Yes.'

'I'll help you. I know most of the plantation owners around here. Who were the purchasers?'

'One was a red-faced man with a big purple nose. He bought my sister Afi.'

He thought for a bit, then said,

'That'd be be old Judge Lovelace. He has a big manor house just outside town, near the Assembly.'

'I didn't get a good look at the other one. He was tall and thin with a hat like a big, black chimney.'

'That could be anyone. I'll tell you what: I'll drop you off at the Judge's place. I have to pass it anyway.'

Abena was glad she'd shared her secret with this cheery soul. Now she'd be reunited with Afi and, together, they'd go in search of their mother. As the mule cart approached a large white-stone house, the mule driver pointed ahead.

'That's Judge Lovelace's mansion. I've a brother working in those tobacco fields. He might know about your sister. Wait here and keep your head down.'

He pulled up beside a low fence, just in front of a clump of trees. Jumping down, he ran off in the direction of some thatched huts.

Abena breathed a sigh of relief. She trusted the young slave. After all, if he were discovered aiding an escaped slave, he could be in trouble himself.

About half an hour went by before she spotted half a dozen men running up the road. Only when she realised they were making for the cart did she grow alarmed. Quickly, she leapt out and took to her heels. But she was no match for the men who soon overtook her, pinned her arms behind her back and frogmarched her to the manor house. There, the man with the purple nose was waiting.

When Abena saw the Judge hand money to her 'friendly' mule driver, she realised she'd been betrayed. Runaway slaves evidently had a price on their heads.

She was flung into an outhouse and left under lock and key without food or drink until the following morning. Then she was taken by the same mule driver, trussed up like a chicken, back to Orange River Estate. She knew the fate of runaway slaves: either they had their feet cut off, or were slowly grilled over a fire until they died.

But the Master had a whole range of what he called his 'little amusements'. She was forced into a cage like a captive wild animal, and kept there for two days and nights. Squatting in a corner, she stared with hatred as the house-slaves came and went, none of them daring to approach her.

The Master even sent someone to poison her – but she scornfully refused the food, spitting at him like a wild cat. On the third day, a brown-black man came to unlock the cage. But instead of setting her free or barbecuing her, the man hauled her to a wooden post in the yard. While he held her upright, another man hammered a long nail through her right ear into the post.

Now she could scarcely move her head at all without terrible pain, she hadn't eaten for four days, her throat was parched and her body stank of dried filth. Not a single person raised a finger to help her.

Forty-three

Mungo saw that Peggy was not easy to break in. She took to her duties as reluctantly as a kitten to water. No matter how often Molly warned her she dragged her feet, working slowly and unwillingly. There was little anyone could do to shield her from the Master's wrath. Yet the more he beat her, the less she screamed and the slower she worked.

One day she disappeared. No one knew where. She just upped and went – perhaps in search of her mother and sister. Who knows? How Mungo hoped she'd make it to safety! He couldn't bear to think what punishment awaited her if she got caught. Maybe she'd have her feet chopped off, like Kwasi.

However, he had enough on his hands, what with Hetty's whims and caprices, and just lately a fever had struck her down. She was grumpier than ever, demanding Mungo's presence round the clock.

Three days after Peggy's disappearance, Molly announced to a hushed kitchen that the girl had been captured and locked up in the Cage. Now, the Cage was a torture chamber of the Master's own devising: it was too small to stand up in and too narrow to lie down in, and the victim was exposed to sun, wind and rain in the yard.

Full of admiration for the young rebel, Mungo stole out at dusk to take a look. She crouched in one corner of the cage, squatting in her own filth and covered in festering cuts. But there was still a spark of defiance in her eyes, like a lioness waiting to spring. She reminded Mungo of the black pirate boy beside the scaffold, suspicious of everyone and full of fear. Since she spoke no English, he couldn't reassure her he was on her side; so he poked some bread and banana through the bars. She refused to touch the food or even to look at it; her eyes were fixed on Mungo's every movement, as if by watching him she might find a way to escape.

'Right sorry I am, girlie,' he said in sympathetic tones. 'You can't swim back to Africa, so there's no point in trying to escape. It'll only end in disaster.'

She stared at him in contempt, as if she were the free creature and he the chained animal.

He turned away.

Next morning, Mungo found her in the yard, nailed by one ear to a wooden post. She could barely move her head. Thus she remained all day, starved of food and drink. In full view of comers and goers, Mungo didn't dare risk slipping her food. He decided to get up early next morning and take her some milk and mango.

Yet when he approached the wooden post at dawn's first glimmering, he was in for a shock. She had gone. Nailed to the post was a bloody scrap of ear.

Where had she fled to this time? Surely, if she were caught again, she'd be flogged to death!

Then Mungo saw her. To his amazement, she was calmly sweeping the yard, a dock leaf tied to her torn ear by a frond. He couldn't help admiring her. Not only was she brave, she was crafty. He felt she was biding her time, working out a safer plan of action.

In the coming days, Mungo had enough to occupy himself without worrying about Peggy. Hetty had taken to her bed and he was detailed by her desperate father to sit beside her every minute of the day and night. He was to call for assistance if she grew worse.

She did get worse. One morning, he heard the doctor tell the grief-stricken father, 'There's little hope.' She'd caught the same fever as her mother and, though they tried poultices, leeches and mustard plasters, nothing helped. Only Mungo's stories seemed to ease the pain. In a calm, quiet voice he would begin, 'Once upon a time...' and Hetty would smile, curl her fingers tightly round his thumb and close her eyes as he told her *The Tale of the Three Little Pigs, Beauty and the Beast* or *Goldilocks and the Three Bears*.

Sometimes, when he thought she'd drifted off to sleep, he'd give his tongue a rest. But she would surprise him by opening her eyes, imploring him by her look to carry on.

There were times when she'd wake up, full of life and eager to talk.

'Mullins,' she once said in the middle of the night. 'Will you ever marry?'

The question brought him out of his cat-nap.

'Uh, no, er, yes, I suppose…'

'Who will you marry?'

'Uh, I haven't really thought.'

'I'm going to marry a rich man, a handsome gentleman, an officer.'

He smiled. 'And live on a big plantation?'

'Oh no! I hate this place. I shall live in a grand house in England. I'll go riding in the morning, sleep in the afternoon, and have balls and parties every night.'

Her eyes sparkled with a feverish glow: just for a moment she was picturing herself as lady of the manor. Then the glow faded and she returned to Mungo.

'Mullins, you'll marry a domestic.'

That stung him.

'Maybe I will, maybe I won't,' he said, blushing. 'I might marry a slave.'

'What? A black woman! You can't!'

'Why not?'

She was so appalled at his reply that she was at a loss for an answer.

'You just can't! Because… because… you won't

see her in the dark.'

He laughed so loudly at this, she even giggled herself.

'Well, she won't see me in daylight – so we'll never see each other.'

She lay back on the pillow and went off to sleep with a smile on her face.

Even though he was starved of sleep, he did his best to keep awake, snatching rest moments as her father or the doctor sat by her side. In the middle of one night, she suddenly sat up and said clearly,

'I spoke to Mummy. She says it's time to go.'

Then she fell back, and never opened her eyes again.

Mr Trelawny was heart-broken and for several weeks wasn't seen around the house at all. Now and then, his drunken bellowing would echo through the empty rooms, and his sobbing could be heard as far away as the row of shacks. Mungo, lying in Kwasi's hut, could hear it. Peggy, in Phibia's old hut, could hear it. Neither had any pity for a father's grief.

Mungo pondered over the tragedy of the Master's life. No family. No friends. No one to trust, afraid of being poisoned by his slaves. It was a race against time: either to make his fortune and return to England, or to die of disease like his wife and daughter. It was sad to watch the little mite die and Mungo felt genuinely sorry for her. Yet how much sorrier he felt for the slaves her father tormented and killed without so much as batting an eyelid.

At the bottom of the garden stood a marble slab put up by the previous owner of Orange Tree Estate. It marked the resting-place of eight young children aged from three weeks to fourteen years. The master himself had died last of all, after his wife, at the ripe old age of fifty-two; Jamaica proved to be the graveyard of many white hopes of making a quick fortune.

Even in his short time on the island, Mungo had learned the sad irony of its people. There were two distinct groups: masters and slaves, both strangers to the land on which they met. Both despised, distrusted and loathed each other. Only the chains of slavery and the crack of the whip kept them together. But it was poor binding material. They had nothing in common, so it was a brittle, fragile society constantly on the brink of disaster.

'What'll become of us?' Mungo asked Kwasi that evening.

'Who knows? If we black heathens could descend to Hell, the Master would most likely blame us for his daughter's death and send us there. Even if he drinks himself to an early grave, we'll be sold off, maybe to an even crueller master, or an absentee landlord, and left to the whim of drivers and overseers.'

'Don't you ever dream of being free?' asked Mungo.

'I did once. Not now. I long for death: when I die, I'll return to my home far away, to my own soil, my own gods.'

Mungo felt sorry for this gentle, proud man.

'You're old,' Mungo sighed. 'But I'm young. I can't wait that long; nor can poor Peggy. That's clear enough.'

Mungo saw that Kwasi had taken an interest in the new slave girl. There was evidently something about her that appealed to him. He wondered why, since she spoke to no one.

The old man suddenly said, 'You seem to get on with her. Why not ask her along after work? I might be able to talk to her.'

Mungo threw up his hands.

'She's like a sore-headed crocodile! She'd peel off my skin and chew me up like a banana if she had half a chance.'

All the same, he tried. That day, after work, he stuck close as Peggy walked back to her hut. And, by gestures, he indicated the old man with one hand, and his mouth with the other.

'Talk – yak-yak-yak...' he said, making hand movements.

'Peggy – Mungo – Kwasi...'

She ignored him until he spoke the name 'Kwasi'. She hesitated, repeating it a few times: 'Kwa – si. Kwa – si, Kwa – si...' Then she shrugged her thin shoulders and stepped slowly towards their hut. She wouldn't enter, just stood outside, hands on hips, with a furtive look around to see no one was listening.

Kwasi came out and spoke to her in a tongue Mungo didn't understand. The words were low murmurs in sing-song tones, like gusts of wind humming and sighing in the trees. But the girl suddenly came to life; the sullen, angry look melted away and she nodded or shook her head, with a dull glow in her eyes.

Now it was her turn to speak: a mellifluous tumble of words, with occasional growls. At one moment she seemed to grow angry and flung the word 'Pe-ggee' at him, repeating over and over again something that sounded like 'O-pen-oh' or 'A-pen-oh'. After a few moments the conversation ceased and she turned on her heel, stepping briskly back to her hut.

When Kwasi and Mungo were alone, the old man explained.

'We're not the same people. But I know enough of her language to communicate. Like most of us, she's from the Gold Coast. Whites call us Coromantines after the chief shipping port there. We speak one of the Akan languages – they're related, but not the same.'

Mungo didn't understand.

'I thought you all spoke the same language.'

Kwasi laughed. 'Like you Europeans, you mean?'

Mungo felt ashamed.

'Africa is far bigger than Europe, lad; with as many languages as there are stars in the sky. As many gods. As many wars. As many ways of life. As many shades of brown and black. Most slaves are from the Gold Coast, so some of us have words in common. But the white masters forbid us to speak in our own tongue.'

He paused, and a smile spread over his face.

'So most slaves talk a garbled English learned from poorly-educated sailors and overseers; this we turn into a language that only we can understand. You've heard field workers singing – can you catch the words?'

'No,' Mungo had to admit.

'That's *our* language. We sing of Africa and freedom, pass on information to rebels, and poke fun at the whites. And all the while the overseers think we're singing spiritual songs!'

'What did you and the girl talk about?' asked the boy.

'Home. Family. Slavery. She hates the name "Peggy" as much as I do "Old Bones".'

'What's her real name?'

'Abena.'

Forty-four

That night, Mungo found sleep hard to capture, despite heavy eyelids and an aching body. The bright moon formed a round pool of light on the floor. It was a muggy night that brought midges and mosquitoes out to play; their humming above his head was fraying Mungo's nerves.

But there was something else.

It had to be coincidence. 'Abena' was likely a common African or, rather, Akan name – like 'Jane' or 'Rose' or 'Harry' in England.

Across the room, Kwasi too was restless. The boy heard the occasional swipe at pestering insects and angry curses in that same language he'd spoken earlier. The rebel girl had obviously stirred up half-forgotten memories.

It was the boy who broke the silence.

'Mr Kwasi, that girl… you know, ah, Abena. Is that a usual name, er, where you come from?'

The old man gave a grumpy snort – at having to teach the boy the facts of life.

'I was born on a Sunday, so Kwasi's my given name. In Akan and Ashanti alike. Sunday girls are Akosua. Tuesday boys are Kwabena, girls Abena. Simple enough: your name's your birthday, like saints' name days among whites.'

'Oh.'

'Why do you ask?'

Mungo made up his mind. It was time to entrust to his companion the story of the black pirate boy. Fetching the scrap of parchment from its hiding-place inside the straw palliasse, Mungo spread it on the earthen floor in the pool of moonlight. Kwasi peered closely and murmured in surprise.

'Well, well. Interesting. In the right hands that sketch could be useful. No idea about the name. Whoever wrote it must be from Ashanti lands.'

'It has *her* name on it,' said Mungo.

'Yes, and that of thousands of other girls born on a Tuesday!'

Mungo slipped the paper back into its cache, and the two of them lapsed into silence, each with his own thoughts.

Next day, Mungo had no chance to question the girl. He learned from Mulatto Molly that she'd been assigned other duties – to the sugar factory where women fed the sugar mill that crushed syrup out of the cane, squeezing it into great bubbling vats.

Abena wasn't the only one to have new duties. Now that his nanny responsibilities were at an end, Mungo found himself the new yard boy. He was pleased to have a fresh air job – sweeping the yard, feeding the chickens and collecting their eggs, looking after the thoroughbreds in the paddock. The last chore was like old times, grooming Josh and Bessie.

Since the yard was his territory, he had to witness the many floggings for crimes and misdemeanours, real or otherwise. More than once he saw black flesh made ragged and raw. After Hetty's death, Mr Trelawny turned into a more brutal, drunken tyrant than ever.

Even Molly, his favourite, who was now pregnant, didn't escape the Master's vengeance. One day, a cow broke loose, having dragged the rope away from the stake to which Molly had tied it. The Master ordered Molly stripped and tied to a ladder in the yard before he started the whipping. He continued until she was streaming blood. Her shrieks were terrible to hear. Not long after, she lost the baby.

That wasn't the worst Mungo had to watch. Slaves had their ears lopped off, noses slit, their Achilles tendons severed, their feet and even their right leg chopped off to prevent them running away again. One poor woman was tied to a tree for a week with a loaf of bread hanging before her mouth. She starved to death.

One day, Mungo saw a young girl being hauled up by a rope to the branch of a tree in the yard – so that only her toes touched the ground. The entire weight of her body rested on her wrists and the tips of her toes. At the time, he was feeding the horses in the paddock, so mercifully he saw the scene from a distance.

Only when he was returning an hour later did he recognise the girl.

Abena!

No one dared approach... under threat of receiving the same punishment.

It was one of the water carriers, Congo Nancy, who told Mungo, 'She caught her fingers in the rollers. Two were crushed.'

Mungo didn't understand.

'What was her crime?'

'Her blood spoiled the sugar juice.'

'How long will she hang there?' Mungo asked Nancy.

'Till she dies,' replied Nancy matter-of-factly.

As Nancy staggered off with her full pitchers of water, Mungo stared pitifully at poor Abena. Only a ragged white cloth covered her. Her wrists were tied together by rope hanging from a branch, her head drooped to one side, and blood dripped down from her crushed fingers. The toes of one foot touched the ground, while the other leg was bent at the knee. The pain must have been terrible as she balanced alternately on the tips of her toes.

A pair of mulatto overseers stood by, laughing and poking fun at the girl's distress, while passing house-women averted their gaze. They knew that one slip, one accident, one look that vexed the Master could put them in Peggy's place – or worse.

'What can we do?' Mungo asked Kwasi, back in their hut.

The old African gave the boy a careworn look.

'Mind our own business.'

Mungo was surprised. Had Kwasi's fighting spirit been knocked out of him?

'Don't you care?' he said. 'She's almost your own flesh and blood!'

Kwasi bowed his head.

'Of course I care,' he mumbled after a while. 'But what can we do?'

Mungo was thinking about the stories of runaway slaves living in the mountains.

'We could run away.'

With a sigh, the old man shrugged.

'Runaway blacks are easy to spot. She wouldn't get far.'

'But if she could reach the hills, she'd be safe...'

'They'd set the hounds on her before she got that far, call out the militia. Runaways are the biggest challenge to white authority. How could a lone, branded black girl evade dogs and soldiers?'

'She wouldn't be alone,' cried Mungo. 'I'm going with her!'

Forty-five

Kwasi stared at the young boy. Slowly a grin spread over his wrinkled features and a spark of the old defiance appeared in his rheumy eyes.

'Bush, bush, have no law...' he chanted. 'Take to the bush, eh?'

He paused to think about it. When he spoke, his words surprised Mungo.

'Take me with you. You'll need my help.'

Mungo admired the old African's courage. It was true, he could do with a go-between and guide. But Kwasi would slow them up, and time was vital if they were to escape trackers with dogs.

Kwasi went on, 'Running away isn't a foot race. 'Our best chance is to make for rebel villages in the mountains, Nanny's Town, over Carrion Crow Hill. We'll have to find a way through vines and creepers in the foothills.'

He smiled ruefully. 'I may not be able to run, but I can follow hidden tracks into the hills.'

Mungo still wasn't convinced. He looked with pity at the old man: no ears, no toes, no teeth. Still, he knew the bush, that was for sure.

'All right,' he said slowly. 'But it'll have to be

tonight, after the nine o'clock curfew. The poor girl might peg out by morning.'

'You're right. Take my knife and cut her down. Then bring her here so she can rest before we set off. We need a head start on the search party.'

Mungo tucked the knife into the top of his breeches and left the hut.

It was early March and grey clouds tinged with violet were rolling across the sky, playing hide-and-seek with the full moon. Low growls of thunder rent the air like a guard dog's warning. Close on their heels came jagged lightning. It was misty and cold, but the rain held off.

Mungo skirted the back of the huts, keeping to the shadows of buildings – round the big house, past the wash-house and buttery, in and out of the coach-house posts, crouching low past the chicken coop. He was heading for the cluster of trees that stood in the centre of the yard.

Hopefully, the domestics would be asleep and the Master snoring in a drunken stupor. No one could be seen apart from the slim figure hanging lopsidedly from the tall casuarina tree fringed in horse-tails. Mungo's biggest fear was that Ben, the chained guard dog, would raise the alarm. But dog and boy knew each other well since it was Mungo who fed the beast, and he'd now brought some bones from the stew-pot.

While Ben slavered over the bones, Mungo stole

towards the tree, carrying a stool in one hand and Kwasi's knife in the other. For a moment, he thought he was too late. The body hung limp and lifeless.

'Abena!' he called as loudly as he dared. Ben growled menacingly.

No movement. No flicker. No response.

Standing on the stool, he cut through the rope tying her wrists together; then he proceeded to saw through the tougher, thicker strands connected to the overhanging branch. Her body slumped to the ground with a sickening thud.

She let out a long moan and half-opened her eyes. Bringing Mungo into focus, she cowered back, as if trying to press her body into the earth. All he could do was put a finger to his lips, calling softly, 'Abena – Kwasi, Abena – Kwasi.' She seemed to understand, for she forced herself up on all fours and started crawling away from the tree.

'No, no. You, me, Kwasi. Run away. To the hills.'

He made signs of running and pointed towards the dim outline of the Blue Mountains. Then he helped her up, putting one of her skinny arms round his neck so as to take most of her weight. She put up no resistance.

He felt a thrill of excitement run through him. At that moment he was closer to the young black girl than to any white person. And he was going to run away with her. Even if they were caught – Heaven forbid! – he'd have struck a blow for freedom, fought back against the evil slave system.

Together they staggered from the yard just as large dollops of rain began to fall. Somehow the boy managed to half-lift, half-drag her to the hut where Kwasi was waiting. They laid her down on the straw bed, with Kwasi murmuring calming words to take her mind off the pain, and fed her mashed plantain and milk.

The old man was obviously explaining their escape plan, for she was nodding. What soon became apparent, however, was that, unless they were to carry her, she wouldn't be going anywhere. Her feet were swollen, her mauve hands unable to grasp the tin mug of milk; her wounds clearly needed time to heal.

'What are we to do?' Mungo asked desperately.

'She can't stay here,' said Kwasi. 'With my reputation, it's the first place they'll look.'

'We must hide her somewhere, at least till she's fit enough to walk.'

It was Abena herself who supplied an answer. From a tumble of words that issued from her, between wild grimaces of pain, Kwasi translated.

'She says there's a woman she knows in a field hut nearby. If we can get her there, she'll be safe for a few days. It'll give her time to recover. Hopefully the rain will wash away her scent.'

Mungo nodded. There was no alternative.

Kwasi hobbled ahead to warn the woman, Annie,

while Abena rested for an hour or so to recover the use of her arms and legs. When she was finally able to stand, Mungo helped her to walk, then rest, walk some more, rest. Stop-start. It took a couple of hours before, eventually, the girl was safely transferred to a small hut on the edge of the cane fields.

Luckily, Annie was also skilled in bush medicine. Gently, she washed and smeared Abena's wounds with a paste made from crushed pods, then covered them with broad green leaves. The potion she forced down Abena's throat seemed to cool the fever.

Next morning there was a great hullabaloo at the mansion. Fortunately for the intending runaways, it was the middle of crop time when work was at its most frenzied, and no one could be spared for a search party. If anyone was to pursue the quarry, it'd have to be the militia – and that would take time. In any case, today was Sunday, rest day for God-fearing white folk. Despite his rage, the Master had to put off arrangements for the hunt until he'd sung hymns and prayed to his god.

Mungo was roped in for church-going. The Master wanted to interrogate him during the forty-minute ride to church. With Old Bones up front, Mr Trelawny sat Mungo opposite, bouncing about on leather cushions.

'What d'you know, you Irish scum? Did you cut her down? Did you help her pull foot? I wouldn't put it past you, you ginger scallywag! As Christ's my witness,

I'll cut her into a thousand pieces when I get my hands on her!'

Mungo was forced to swear on Mr Trelawny's old leather Bible that he knew nothing. It didn't matter to him whether he swore on a pile of horse manure: he had no intention of giving Abena away or signing his own and Kwasi's death warrant.

At the white hilltop chapel, the Master took his seat in the front pew alongside other respectable gentlemen, while Mungo was made to sit at the back, next to other dregs of white society – mostly house-servants.

The parson, a tall, lean man with shiny pink pate and sharp elbows who minced about like an eaglet trying to fly, stood in a pulpit above the congregation of some forty or more plantation owners and domestics. He announced that the theme of the sermon would be 'The White Man's Burden'. After a couple of hymns and the Lord's Prayer, he got into his stride.

Mungo gazed about him: he looked first at the pious, saintly faces of the congregation, then up at the parson's earnest figure. Clearly, they all believed deeply and sincerely in their God-sent mission. And they listened intently to the godly words of the Reverend Shuttleworth.

'My fellow Christians, by removing Africans from the Dark Continent, where cannibalism and heathen sorcery are rampant, we are doing them a favour...

'There are those who frown upon what they call the tyranny of slavery. But, brethren, let me tell you this: surely God ordained slaves for our use and benefit. His Divine Will would have been made manifest by some sign or token if he thought otherwise...

'Africans are, I assure you, a lower form of animal, sent by God. Let us not doubt that every member of creation is wisely fitted and adapted to certain uses, and confined within certain bounds to which it is ordained by the Divine Fabricator...'

Mungo rolled the words around his mind: 'Divine Fabricator... God ordained... Divine Will... White Man's beasts of burden...' But what did they mean – that slavery was all fine and good if God said so?

But did He? Where was it written in the Bible? Where did it say that white people had the right to make slaves of Africans and treat them like dogs? The parson gave no clue.

However, from the devout looks of satisfaction on the fleshy faces of the gentlemen and their ladies, all seemed to agree that it was a fine sermon.

Forty-six

As Abena stood nailed to the post, her hatred for the house-servants grew with every figure who hurried past, eyes averted. Were these lackeys so afraid for their own skin that they dared not disobey the Master and help a fellow African? How could her own people turn into such cringing, cowardly lickspittles?

As night fell and everyone went to bed, she grew more and more angry. If nobody would help her, she'd have to rely on herself. Her resolution to break free rose apace with her fury and frustration. At first she tried to pull out the nail with her fingers, but it was too well driven into the post. She then attempted to draw her ear along the nail; but the nail head was too broad.

Finally, in a temper, she tore herself away from the post, leaving half her ear on the nail.

'*Aiy-eee-eee-eee!*'

The pain was agonising. She slapped her right hand against the bleeding ear to staunch the blood and ease the agony. Staggering about, driven crazy by pain, she gritted her teeth and picked a dock leaf to make a compress on her ear, binding it with fibre. It was only a temporary respite. She made for the buttery, flung open the door and peered about in the half-light from a full moon. In the middle of the outhouse was a big vat where they churned milk into butter and cheese.

Smearing butter from the vat over the raw wound, she drank some of the whey and pushed fingerfuls of cream and cheese into her mouth. It made her feel sick, but at least the liquid lubricated her throat and eased the aching in her stomach.

What was she to do now? Run away again? In her weak state, she wouldn't get far. No, she needed to bide her time and wait for the ear to heal.

It amused her to see how surprised the house-slaves were in the morning to notice her free and calmly sweeping the yard. Even the Master was taken aback. Instead of punishing her, he gave her a hut to sleep in and let her sweep the yard until he'd decided what to do with her.

So Abena worked and watched, not speaking to anyone until one day, as dusk was falling, the Red Boy who'd tried to poison her followed her back to the hut. He kept smacking his mouth and gobbling like a turkey-cock, pointing to the old African buggy-driver standing outside a hut. She ignored the stupid boy until he uttered the name 'Kwa-si'. Was he really speaking a word familiar to her? She repeated it to make sure: 'Kwasi, Kwasi.' That made him smile and nod, saying, 'Yess-ss, yess-ss.'

What did they want with her, this red-haired boy and the old black man, one who gobbled, the other who never spoke? Out of curiosity, she stepped towards the hut into which the old man had disappeared.

To Abena's amazement, the old fellow emerged, speaking in a low, beautiful voice, words she could understand, even though they weren't in her own tongue. What pleased her most was when he said he rejected his slave name: he was *Kwasi*, not 'Old Bones'. She immediately flung the word 'Peggy' at him, saying she would always be Abena. She told him her story.

'You're a brave girl,' he said.

After a few weeks as yard girl, she was taken by the slave Ama-Annie to work in the sugar mill – what Ama called 'the Factory'. The Master had been lenient, thinking to drown her frenzy in hard work: even the most savage of creatures could be tamed by toil.

'You're lucky,' said Ama, as they made their way towards a long house on the edge of the cane fields.

'Lucky to be a slave?' said Abena with a sneer.

'Lucky to be alive. Anyone who defies the Master is usually put to death.'

'Death is better than being a slave!'

Ama saw there was no point arguing. When they reached the Factory, she opened the door into what at first looked like a long cow shed, with a paved corridor down the middle. On one side, enveloped in tall plumes of steam, black women were feeding cane into rollers at one end, while others pushed them into a grinding machine that extracted the juice. At the far end, the dried cane dropped through the floor and was taken away as trash, for fuel.

The noise and smell made Abena's head throb and ears ring. Added to the juddering, clacking rhythm of the rollers and the tearing, pounding racket of the grinder, there was a bubbling, hissing noise of sugar boiling in great copper vats. From these vats came an overpowering, sickly-sweet smell that pervaded the entire mill. Opposite the rollers, grinders and vats were trenches in which men were raking grains of brown sugar as they dried out, rather like sand upon a shore when the tide went out.

Ama had to put her mouth against Abena's good ear to be heard above the din.

'All new girls start on the rollers. Watch your fingers!'

She left Abena to it.

The work wasn't hard to start with. But Abena could see from the women's tired, leathery faces and sluggish movements that once you'd been up since five, toiling all morning, your arms and back ached as if lifting ten-ton weights. What with the hot steam and sickly stench, she soon started to feel light-headed.

Perhaps it was being unused to the atmosphere that made her careless. As she dropped a bundle of cane on to the rollers, one end snagged in her shirt. She tugged it free, tearing her shirt and pushing the cane crossly into the rollers. In so doing, she jammed her fingers between two of the metal rollers beneath the cane.

Abena let out a shriek that could be heard above the din. Within seconds, an overseer had shut off the power and halted the whole production line. Just in time – before her hand was chewed up by the machine! She quickly withdrew her fingers: the top of her middle finger was missing, and two others were mangled. She stared at her crushed hand above the rollers, blood dripping down.

Instead of helping her, the overseer, his face twisted with fury, struck her several times, knocking her to the stone floor. Next thing she knew, she was being dragged feet first over the paving stones and out of the door. She was left sprawled on the ground.

It was Ama-Annie who once again took care of her. This time she lost patience with the stupid girl.

'You spoilt the sugar!' she yelled, as if that were the greatest sin on earth. 'You're for it this time!'

Wrapping her crushed fingers in her discarded shirt, Abena staggered to her feet and shuffled after Ama to learn her fate. Evidently, spoiling sugar was a far worse crime than running away…

Once back at the house, a brawny overseer tied her wrists together before dragging her to a tree in the middle of the yard. There he hauled her up by a rope to an overhanging branch so that only her toes touched the earth. It was a cunning and cruel punishment that led to an inevitable slow, agonising end. The entire weight of her body hung from her wrists and rested on her toes. She was to hang like that, a lesson to others, until the last breath passed from her body.

Gradually her waking moments became fewer and fewer, shorter and shorter. As night fell, so her own darkness descended and she lapsed into a pain-filled sleep in which she longed for death. Her last, silently-uttered words were for her mother and sister. No longer 'We shall survive!', but, 'Farewell, Mama... Farewell, Afi....'

In her pain-racked slumber she suddenly felt a sharp blow. It was as if she possessed two bodies – one hanging lifeless from the tree, the other being cut down to be buried. In the distance, she heard someone muttering 'Abena-Kwasi' (why Kwasi?); someone was jumping up and down and pointing. Then she felt one of her bodies being carried away – no doubt to be buried in Africa.

Next thing she knew, she was lying on a straw mat, being fed and hearing soothing words in her native tongue. Was she alive or not? As the food warmed her stomach, she slowly brought into focus the old African and the red-haired boy. They were talking to her, they were planning to run away to the hills – and she was going with them!

When she finally found her voice, she told them of Ama-Annie, who might hide her until she was fit to walk again.

But Kwasi and the boy (whose name was Mungo –
it sounded like a slave name!) were impatient to leave.
As soon as she could walk, they would begin their
escape, in the middle of the night, the three of them.

It was hopeless: a boy, an old man whose feet had
been cut in half, and a girl with half an ear, three
mangled fingers and a body as weak as a kitten.

Forty-seven

News of the empty 'hanging tree' went round the estate like wildfire. While the owner and his manager were convinced the slave girl had run, there were mutterings among the slaves of magic spirits and the supernatural...

Whatever they believed, every slave and domestic rejoiced that the young rebel girl had overcome white power. And each swore that no whip could ever cut her skin, no bonds could ever tie her down, no fire could as much as singe her hair. For all of them, Abena was a shining hope.

Even Kwasi, whose knife had severed the ropes and who knew where she was hiding, likened her to the legendary Nanny.

'Folk are saying she possesses magical powers,' he told Mungo, on the boy's return from church. 'She's like Nanny, the *obeah* who gives counsel to the Windward rebels.'

Mungo shook his head. He was as uncertain about black magic and spirits as he was about white gods and the Holy Ghost. But his ears pricked up at the mention of Nanny, the rebel leader.

'Tell me about Nanny, Mr Kwasi. Is she as powerful

as the house-women say?'

'Huh!'

The grunt meant either that the old African didn't hold with Nanny stories, or that he was afraid to invoke the wrath of the spirits.

Mungo had learned to be patient if he wished to hear Kwasi's stories.

At last, when he was ready, the old African cleared his throat and spoke in a voice that came all the way up from his toeless boots.

'Nanny was born to an Ashanti chieftain. So they say, so they say… She lives somewhere in the Blue Mountains, in a village of rebel settlements named after her: Nanny Town. She is a great warrior, wiser than the white *bacarra* parties sent to destroy the rebels. She communes with the spirits and they tell her the best time and place to do battle with English soldiers. So they say, so they say…'

Mungo was sceptical.

'If she's as powerful as they say, how come she hasn't led her army to free all the slaves? Are you sure she exists?'

'Oh yes!' Kwasi's sharp tone betrayed his annoyance. 'If you don't believe black tales, then listen to white stories. There are plenty told by officers sent to capture her. They've always come home with their tails between their legs, full of what they've seen.'

'What have they seen?' asked Mungo.

'One officer said that Nanny's tall and proud and never bows to whites. On her wrists and ankles are bracelets made from the teeth of slain soldiers. And that's not all. She wears a belt with a dozen different knives hanging down, all rusty with English blood. Just the sight of her puts the fear of God into English soldiers, and they run away.

'Another officer actually witnessed her magical powers. When his soldiers fired muskets at her defenders, she stood on a hill and – would you believe – bared her backside at them... And then she drew all the bullets towards her like a magnet, caught them and spat them out like plum stones.'

Mungo tried not to laugh.

'Do you believe the stories?' he asked.

Kwasi clammed up. He clearly wanted to believe in the Ashanti priestess who could defeat the English army. But he was wary of the boy's scorn.

Mungo went on: 'We know it was your knife in my hand that cut Abena down. It wasn't a crow's beak or locust teeth.'

'That's as may be,' Kwasi muttered.

After a lengthy pause, he growled, 'Don't mock what you don't understand, boy!'

Mungo felt it was time to stop talking. Why should he deny people hope? People who had nothing else to feed on? Slaves needed to believe in magic that could save them from pain and suffering. But his scepticism had obviously got under Kwasi's skin.

'Even your white bible-thumpers need their miracles and *obeahs*,' the old man muttered, 'who can raise bodies from the dead.'

It wasn't a matter of blacks being simple-minded or more gullible than whites. As Kwasi wisely said, they both needed their gods, but for different reasons: one to justify slavery, the other to overthrow it. It was just that, having risked his life to save Abena's skin, Mungo resented yarns of crows and locusts.

Mr Trelawny didn't believe in magic either. He had an escaped slave on his hands. Apart from lost revenue, a runaway slave was a challenge to his authority. If one slipped through the net, more could follow, and not just small fry. Of late, slaves had been getting bolder. More and more from all over the island had run away, and bands of marauding rebels had raided and burned down outlying plantations, killing their white owners and overseers. No amount of beatings, amputations and roastings seemed to deter them.

Something had to be done. It was about time the English government took action – before it was too late and slaves took over the island. Time and again, the planters' Assembly and the Governor himself had appealed to the King for help.

Now, at long last, Parliament had sent an expeditionary force of a hundred soldiers to deal with the situation.

When Mr Trelawny took his complaint the following Monday morning to Kingston, he was told that this expeditionary force, with twenty-two black baggage carriers, had already embarked on a cunning plan to wipe out the rebels. Instead of attacking rebel strongholds in the mountains from the south, through thickly-wooded, rocky terrain, the soldiers had sailed from Port Royal round to Plum Tree Bay in the north. They would make a surprise attack on rebel positions from the rear, where they least expected it. Their mission was to flush the rebels out of their mountain hideaways and clear more land for new plantations.

That did not satisfy Mr Trelawny, as he told the Governor in no uncertain terms.

'March is the very height of the sugar harvest. It will be May at least before the army moves into action. I need action now to catch my slave. If she gets away scot-free, others will follow. I can't afford to lose a single pair of hands at crop-time.'

In the end, he had to be content with a white militiaman and two mulatto trackers with a pack of bloodhounds, and by Thursday, he had put together his hunting party.

Mungo, Kwasi and Abena had a day's start. But, while the pursuers' progress would be swift, the fugitives could only move slowly. Three days had passed since Abena had been cut down. She was still weak, but could hobble along with the aid of a stick.

Her thin body was covered with festering sores and half-exposed cuts.

Kwasi, too, could barely hobble over the flat savanna land to the north east of the estate. Only Mungo was in a fit state to make a bid for freedom.

They started out at first light on Wednesday, intending to live off fruit, roots, nuts and water along the way. The only witnesses to their flight were the herds of steers, cows and mules grazing peacefully in meadows which the fugitives had to cross to reach the rutted hill road.

Since he knew the lie of the land, Kwasi had mapped out the path they were to follow:

'Yallahs River into the hills up to Hobby's Plantation. From there we climb Carrion Crow Hill to Stoddards Peak, following Snake River down into the Rio Grande Valley. By then, we should be close to rebel settlements.'

It sounded simple enough...

But, thought Mungo, even if they did make it to safety, what then? What if the rebels regarded him – the only white person among them – as likely to give away their positions? It would be a case of *bang-bang-bang*, no questions asked.

The early morning air was fresh and moist as they made their way through meadowy glades and tough grass. Animals grazing in the stock pens gazed at them with mild curiosity. All at once, as they were passing a pen full of pack mules, Kwasi let out a shout:

'Mules! We'll borrow Mr Trelawny's mules!'

Easier said than done. It took half their supply of bananas before they'd roped in a couple of very unwilling mules. But the beasts of burden certainly eased the pain of walking for Kwasi and Abena. With the whack of sticks and the persuasion of more bananas, the mules reluctantly bore their riders to the track running into the lower mountain slopes. Once on the road, the going was somewhat easier, though the higher they climbed along a marl track of beaten clay and lime, fringed by wooded chasms, the more they found their way blocked by fallen rocks and trees. At one spot, they had to splash through a ford over the Great Gully.

'Our first real obstacle,' said Kwasi, 'is Hobby's Plantation. Its absentee-owner, Sir Montague Cotton, is probably sitting cosily in his country house near Bristol. But his estate manager will show no mercy to runaways. He has look-outs posted all round the plantation. So keep your eyes peeled!'

Forty-eight

All the three fugitives could do was hope they weren't stopped. There was no other way into the mountains. One side was a sheer drop on to jagged rocks in the gully below; the other was a steep limestone cliff that no man or beast could climb.

So far, so good. Not a soul was seen all morning. But their luck did not hold. In the late afternoon, they were spotted by a rider just as they thought they'd safely skirted Hobby's Plantation. The man fired a shot into the air and came galloping after them.

'Halt, or I'll pepper your black hides with gunshot!'

Only when he caught up with them did the man realise his mistake. Mungo's pale skin and ginger hair stood out clearly against the grey limestone rock face.

'Where's your pass, boy?' The question was addressed to Kwasi.

Mungo anwered.

'They need no pass,' he shouted. 'They're in my care. I'm Mr Trelawny's accountant. Take a look, they've his initials branded on them.'

The man hesitated.

'You've a wee head for totting up figures,' he said suspiciously.

'Aye, I'm new. But I've a good head for figures. Try me.'

The man declined the offer.

'Where are you headed?' he barked. 'This road leads nowhere.'

'Mr Trelawny needs some sacks of marl for fertilising. The richest marls are to be found higher up, he reckons.'

'Mmmm. That's true enough, though danged if I know why he's bothered.'

The rider seemed unconvinced. With a flick of the reins, he manoeuvred his horse towards the two mule riders, inspecting their brands and looking out for goods they might have stolen from their master. Finding nothing suspicious, he growled, 'Pretty poor specimens for lugging fertiliser.'

'That's all we can spare at crop-time,' said Mungo, with a shrug. 'You know yourself, sir; men, women, children, day and night, rushing to get the sugar in before it spoils.'

That struck a chord.

'You're right there, matey. I'd better whip my own rogues into shape or they'll be slacking. All right. Good luck.'

Breathing a sigh of relief as the man galloped away, Mungo and his companions pressed on, head down, leading the mules up the mountain track. No one uttered a word until they were well clear of the estate.

'Phew, that was a close shave!' the boy said, wiping his face on his shirt. 'You see, Mr Kwasi, whites have their uses sometimes.'

'Huh!' grunted the old African. 'It takes a thief to know one.' All the same, a broad smile spread over his wrinkled face.

'Time we found shelter for the night. As far as I recall, there's a cave up here somewhere on the right. It looks as if Abena's all in. Riding makes the bottom sore.'

Mungo wasn't impressed.

'Better a sore bottom than aching bones. My feet are killing me.'

Abena hadn't spoken a word all day. Now, at the sound of her name, the old look of defiance came into her eyes, and she mumbled a few words.

'What's she saying?' asked Mungo.

'She doesn't need rest. She wants to keep going... Oh, and she says thank you for saving our skins.'

They moved on. About fifteen minutes later, Kwasi gave a shout. 'Over there.'

All Mungo could see was a giant thicket towering above them at the side of the track. Leaving the two riders on the road, the boy parted the lofty stalks and pushed through a forest of bamboo. He felt like a tiny dormouse in a cornfield.

What was that?

He strained his ears. From somewhere ahead came

strange sounds – as if crowds of people were talking in low tones, all at once.

Kwasi's voice from behind made him jump.

'That's the Murmuring Brook. The cave is across the stream. I made it to here before they caught up with me many years ago.'

Kwasi thrust ahead of Mungo, and they emerged together on the bank of a stream rushing over a limestone piecrust, babbling and chattering as it flowed on its way.

Mungo saw no cave – just a curtain of lianas and creepers hanging down a wall of solid rock.

'Come,' said Kwasi, taking the boy's arm for support. Together they made their way, slipping and sliding, across the fast-flowing stream to the other bank.

'Lucky it's not the rainy season, or the water'd be over our heads, not up to our waist.'

As he spoke, the old man parted the liana curtain to reveal the opening of a cave sloping down into the rock.

'We should be safe here for the night, Master Mungo. We'll tether the mules to bamboo canes beside the stream. The poor devils will be glad of a rest. Now, go and fetch Abena and the…'

Before he could finish, a sudden noise made them both freeze. The sound of baying dogs echoed up from below…

They were being followed!

Wetting one of the three fingers on his right hand, Kwasi held it up to test the direction of the breeze.

'Unless they stop at Hobby's Way, they could be here in a couple of hours. Quick, we've no time to lose.'

Holding tight to Mungo as they struggled back through the stream and bamboo, Kwasi shouted urgently to the girl. She too had heard the dogs barking. They needed to cover their tracks or the bloodhounds would soon sniff them out.

'We'll have to sacrifice the mules,' said Kwasi with a sigh, 'or they'll give us away. We'll try to put the trackers off our scent by going farther up and leaving the animals, then we'll double back through the stream.'

With Mungo's help, he remounted his mule and led the way. The higher they climbed, the more thickly wooded were the sides of the track. But for the dogs, they could have hidden in the trees and thick undergrowth.

All at once, even before they rounded the next bend, they heard the roar of rushing water. Both mules pricked up their ears and sniffed the damp air. They broke into a trot, eager to slake their thirst in the clear mountain stream. At this spot the fountain spouted up from a pot-hole and gushed in eddies into a little lake beside the path, before careering down the mountain. The riders dismounted and left the mules to drink to their hearts' content in the clear water.

Meanwhile, Kwasi took off his jacket and, telling Mungo to do the same, trailed it over the ground and into the undergrowth opposite the pool. Then he removed his cap and tossed it far out into the trees.

'That should throw them off our tail,' he muttered. 'Pity I didn't do this before they caught me last time. We live and learn. Now, have a drink and prepare for a swim.'

He gave Abena the same instructions, and soon all three were washing the dust from their bodies and drinking the cool water of the Murmuring Brook. Kwasi allowed the water to sweep him downstream, the two youngsters drifting with the current behind him.

Buffeted by the rushing swell, the three soon found themselves floating past the bamboo thicket. Struggling to their feet, Mungo and Abena helped Kwasi out of the water. The girl was as surprised as Mungo had been at the well-hidden cave.

Holding the curtain up for them to enter, Kwasi said with a grin, 'You see, Mungo, blacks also have their uses.'

Mungo patted him fondly on the arm as he brushed past into the cave.

Bathing in the stream seemed to have revived Abena for, after a short rest, she left the cave to scout for food. While Kwasi gathered dry bracken for bedding,

Mungo set out to explore the cave. In the darkness he had to feel his way carefully, for the floor was uneven and abruptly sloped down into what appeared to be an underground cavern.

He had taken only a few cautious steps when he realised he wasn't alone.

Forty-nine

Just ahead of him someone... or something... was moving stealthily about; he could hear stones being trodden on and rasping noises.

'Hell – oo – oo-oo!'

No reply. All was silent apart from the tremors of his voice echoing back off the walls. He took a couple of paces forward... and then it struck! Sharp teeth sank into his canvas breeches.

'Owwww!'

He lashed out blindly with his feet, connecting with a solid, squirming mass that fled, hissing, down the dark tunnel. Mungo didn't stop to investigate: he rushed back the way he'd come, flying out of the cave like a bat out of hell.

'There's s-s-someone, d-down there!' stuttered the boy. 'It grabbed me by the seat of my pants – must have taken a great lump out of my backside.'

Mungo pulled down his breeches to examine the wound.

'I can't see any blood,' muttered Kwasi. 'But your precious paper is all chewed up.' The old man looked closer, pulling Mungo's sketch out from the fallen breeches.

'This parchment saved your life,' he said sombrely. 'But for that and your breeches, you'd be a goner. Those are the fang marks of a poisonous snake.'

Mungo strained his neck to catch a glimpse of the red mark on his buttock, already turning to an ugly greeny-yellowy bruise. A girl's voice quickly made him pull up his breeches. Abena was coming towards them, giggling – it was the first time he'd seen her laugh. She said something to Kwasi and they both laughed.

'What's so funny?' asked the boy, reddening.

'She says red-faced boys apparently have red arses too!'

As the girl bent down to release her store of plantains and nuts, she suddenly let out a squeal, pointing to the fallen parchment.

Kwasi translated her rush of words.

'Where did you get that? It's the ship that took my family across the ocean. I drew it myself. Look, my name's there, at the bottom. My brother hid it for safe-keeping...'

Mungo was astonished. But before he could reply, the barking of dogs warned them the trackers were getting nearer.

Poisonous snakes or not, they retreated into the cave and re-covered the entrance as best they could, taking their provisions with them. Only when they were resting on the bracken, backs to the wall, did Mungo relate the story of the black boy. In hushed tones, he told of finding the sketch in the boy's shirt.

'That was my brother Kwame!' said Abena, through Kwasi. 'We were attacked by pirates; they snatched some of the slaves to amuse themselves – throwing some of them to the sharks. I guess Kwame escaped to serve as cabin boy.'

Her eyes shone with excitement at the news of her brother reaching England safely. She assumed that Kwame had given Mungo the sketch.

'Where is my brother?' she asked eagerly.

For several moments Mungo was silent.

'He died in the stable,' he murmured. 'They hanged him, but he escaped badly hurt… We made such plans together. I'm ever so sorry.'

The three of them sat quietly, listening to the gurgling of the wind and occasional shouts from below. It was Mungo who broke the silence.

'Why did you draw rows of slaves?'

'We'd heard about laws against overloading – and our ship had at least four times too many, a good seven hundred bodies when we left Africa. We were hoping to show it to the authorities once we reached land.'

'Humph!'

It was Kwasi.

'A fat lot of good that would have done! The authorities are hand in glove with the slave traders. But… in the right hands, it could still be valuable.'

While Kwasi was translating for Abena, the baying

and shouting rang out no more than a stone's throw away. They could hear what the men were saying.

'Not far ahead…'

'Over here, by the bamboo…'

'No, no, farther up. Come on, over on the other side…'

The voices passed on up the track.

Distant shouts told the hideaways that the men had found the mules. Then came a thrashing and the sharp crack of machetes hacking a way through undergrowth. The high-pitched whine of the lead dog told them the men had uncovered something else.

'Probably my cap,' whispered Kwasi.

About half an hour later, the voices returned, getting louder and louder, and clearly hoarser and angrier. The dogs were whimpering in disappointment.

'Stupid curs!'

Whether the curse was aimed at dogs, mules or runaways, the fugitives could not tell. But then, just as they thought the danger had passed, a splashing close at hand made them hold their breath. From behind the green foliage they made out a mulatto with a dog, wading through the stream and looking in every direction. With hearts racing, they watched as the dog raised its nose right outside the cave.

For what seemed an age, dog and tracker stood stock-still, looking around. A shout from the track disturbed the search.

'Any sign?'

'No. Solid rock beside the stream. Dogs can't pick up the scent in this accursed water.'

'Come on, let's call it off and get back to Hobby's for the night. We'll set off bright and early tomorrow. Without their mules, they won't get far.'

The three spent a restless night. Mungo jumped at the slightest noise. Whenever he dozed off, he saw snakes as big as schooners, their fangs bared, slithering towards him. Once he heard frogs croaking from the stream, followed by a snap and a crunching of bones. He must have dropped off in the early hours, for he awoke with a start, just as a huge snake was about to sink its fangs into his arm.

It was Kwasi shaking him.

The two Africans were already up. They had bathed in the stream, and were now munching a breakfast mash prepared by Abena.

It was still dark as Mungo took a dip in the cool waters, all the while listening out for the dogs. But his splashing was the only sound to be heard against a pre-dawn chorus of frogs and cicadas.

Abena stood leaning on her stick impatiently, waiting for Mungo to dry himself and swallow a few handfuls of food. She gestured for him to hurry, telling him through hand movements that she'd helped Kwasi across the Murmuring Brook and through bamboo to the narrow track; she'd also fashioned a bamboo walking stick for Kwasi to lean on; and now he'd gone on ahead to spy out the land.

Mungo reflected sadly that, from now on, progress would be painfully slow without the mules. Even if Abena was able to walk unaided, Kwasi's infirmity would hold them all up.

A hoarse growl from the girl – 'Munn-ggo-o! Moo-oove yer bloody sel!' – shocked him into action. She must have picked up some choice phrases from the slave ship!

'Coming, Massa!' he cried, wiping his mouth on the back of his hand and leaping up.

She giggled.

He struggled across the stream in her wake; though she'd recovered somewhat from her ordeal, strips of raw pink skin showed clearly on her back in the fading moonlight. Her right ear was seeping blood.

It didn't take them long to catch Kwasi up. Just past the gushing water source they found themselves pushing through thick forest that covered the side of a hill rising up from a vast gorge below. In the breaking dawn, the view was breathtaking.

'That's the Rio Cobre Gorge down there,' explained Kwasi. 'We're climbing Carrion Crow Hill, the lower slopes of the Blue Mountains. Somewhere up there across the ridge' – he threw out an arm – 'is our destination. If we make it, we should be safe.'

Mungo kept his thoughts to himself. He knew it was

a race against time. Even if they made it to a rebel village, would the Bush Rebels welcome a white boy? The more important thought he dare not put into words was that without Kwasi, the two youngsters might just keep ahead of the trackers. But with him...?

Fifty

The old African must have had the same fears, for, at the next resting place, he suddenly said, 'You can make your own way from here.'

Mungo glanced at him sharply.

'What do you mean?'

'The trackers will be on our trail by now, and at our present pace they'll overtake us in a couple of hours. Our only hope is to split up: you and Abena go one way, I'll try to lead them in another. We'll meet at Nanny's Town.'

'What does Abena say?'

Mungo guessed that Kwasi hadn't consulted her.

Kwasi spoke rapidly to the girl. It was obvious what she thought from her angry reaction. She waved her arms about like windmills in a gusty wind, and shook a long, thin finger under his nose. Both of them tried to talk him out of it, peppering him with threats and pleas. But he wouldn't budge. The baying of dogs from below made action urgent. If any of them was to escape, they'd have to move fast – faster than their pursuers

The boy and girl knew full well they were condemning Kwasi to death. As a multiple runaway,

Old Bones was a Wanted Man — dead or alive!

'Get going!' he flung at Mungo, 'or the girl will get killed. They might spare you, but she'll be tortured to death.'

That made up Mungo's mind. Reluctantly, he turned away, took the unwilling Abena by the arm and pulled her through the trees. Neither looked back.

Now the two fugitives made fairly good time, jogging across wooded ridges, clambering over rocks and gullies, and helping each other up steep slopes. After one climb, they stopped briefly, listening to the loud baying and gleeful shouts some way behind them.

They exchanged anxious glances; no words were needed.

Kwasi's capture spurred them on. They had to make it, for his sake. All day long they climbed towards the peak of the Blue Mountains; yet the farther they climbed, the more distant the summit seemed. The effort was beginning to tell on Abena; her pace slowed and finally she sank exhausted to a grassy mound.

'Sling yer 'ook!' she yelled at him – yet another shipboard command. Yet the message was plain enough.

'Wait. I'll find water,' he said, making sipping noises before dashing off to search for rock pools.

He knew the pursuers would have their own stores of water and food, so they wouldn't need delays. He was losing precious time. All the same, he would never abandon the girl. It was because of her that they'd planned the escape in the first place.

His search was futile, apart from some red berries – edible or not, he couldn't tell. While she was squeezing the juice out of them, they could hear the trackers getting closer. Either they'd disposed of Kwasi's body or left someone to guard the prisoner.

Abena hauled herself to her feet and the pair pressed on. Soon they found themselves struggling up a slope between steep hills (the perfect place for an ambush, thought Mungo). A weird sound suddenly echoed around them. It reminded the boy of the conch wake-up call. Yet it had a more eerie, urgent ring to it.

The girl stopped for a moment: it was as if the sound stirred a distant memory in her brain. As they pushed on through the valley, the hollow call merged with a rhythmic beating. If one was a low, extended sigh, the other was an incessant, defiant war chant.

What could it be? Wind rushing through the trees? Distant thunder?

They had no time to stop and wonder. Abena was exhausted, stumbling, falling behind, her breath coming in rasping gasps. The trackers could see their quarry now and were emboldened by the sight. In the middle of a clearing, Abena fell sprawling to the ground and lay still, with only her heaving chest showing signs of life. Looking down, Mungo could see she was bleeding from her re-opened wounds and clearly couldn't walk another step. Shielding her body with his own, he turned to face their pursuers.

The trackers' intentions were brutally obvious. Their instructions must have been to finish the slaves off there and then, for the two mulattos advanced boldly, wielding machetes above their heads. Fear screwed tight Mundo's eyes as he awaited the death blow.

It never came.

All at once, the chorus of hunting horns and drums grew to a deafening din, ringing all round the glade. It halted the attackers in their tracks. As Mungo squinted into the bright sunlight, he saw that the clearing was ringed by a host of black men and women, some with guns, some with spears and machetes, some with bows and arrows.

The Bush Rebels!

The trackers threw down their weapons and raised their hands. One glance confirmed that they couldn't fight their way past a hundred armed warriors; they were swiftly disarmed and their dogs were led away – to serve new masters.

As the boy and girl watched in amazement, an extraordinary figure now entered the clearing. He was short and stocky with a hunched back. But it was his dress that marked him out. He was wearing knee-length pantaloons, an old ragged English army jacket and a rimless black hat. On his right side he carried a cow's horn of powder and a bag of shot, on his left was a broad-sheathed machete hanging from a shoulder strap. His black skin was tinted with red soil, as if he'd risen out of the earth.

'Welcome to freedom!' were his first words in English to the youngsters. 'We've been watching your flight for some hours. You must have heard our *abeng?*'

He motioned towards a hunting horn in the hands of a tall lieutenant.

'Yes, sir,' said Mungo. 'We're grateful to you for saving our lives.'

Not to be ignored, Abena let loose a few gutteral words in Akan, evidently puzzled as to why freed slaves should use the slavers' language. The rebel commander immediately responded in her own tongue. She seemed satisfied.

He shouted to his men farther down the slope, and Mungo and Abena saw a white prisoner being pushed up the hill.

There was no sign of Kwasi. They feared the worst, assuming his body had been ditched in the bush. At long last he was free; now his soul could fly back to its home in Africa.

Meanwhile, thinking their last moment had come, the two mulattos had fallen to their knees, begging for mercy. The commander addressed them sternly.

'Get off your knees, you cowards. No doubt you expect the cruel death you intended for two children and an old man. Unlike you, however, we hold life dear. We kill only to defend our freedom. You are free to go. But... on one condition: we need information about the militia's plans.'

Motioning to his lieutenant, he issued a curt order,

'Take them away and question them. Then let them go unharmed.'

By the time the leader had finished with the prisoners, the rebels had fashioned a stretcher from bamboo sticks bound together with twine. By this means, Abena was borne up the mountain, with Mungo walking beside her.

The rebel commander had not questioned Mungo's right to sanctuary. He seemed unconcerned about his colour. Knowing what black slaves went through, Mungo had assumed that the rebels would hate all whites. And another thing. After suffering the cruellest tortures from their white masters, the rebels could well have given the white militiaman and two mulatto trackers a taste of their own medicine. Yet they'd displayed an uncommon respect for human life.

Yes, mused Mungo, what a pity the chapel bible-thumper isn't here! Who's closer to *Thou Shalt Not Kill* – Christian gentlemen, or so-called savages?

The Bush Rebels marched without a halt until they reached a ridge; and there, not far down the other side, standing on a plateau above a sheer drop, was a collection of wooden huts. The entire settlement was surrounded by a wooden palisade with intermittent rifle slits. The rebels had learned to turn the harshness of the surroundings to their advantage.

The path leading down to the village was carefully disguised, with several false trails and booby traps of pointed spikes covered with leaves, quicksand and quagmires. The narrow defile, wide enough for only a single person, could easily be blocked by boulders at front and rear, while guards overlooked the plateau and the plain in both directions from rock ledges above.

Mungo thanked his lucky stars he had friendly people to guide him – or he'd have surely ended up plunging into a pit full of pointed sticks.

The party was now reduced to ten men and women, since the commander and most of his army had returned to their look-out posts. The two refugees were taken straight to a hut in the centre of the village where they stood awaiting their fate. No one emerged to meet them.

They could hear strange mumblings coming from inside the hut – a high-pitched wail followed by low chanting. Although it sounded like different voices conversing, they guessed it was a medicine man asking the spirits what was to be done with the newcomers.

Suddenly, there was an awesome silence and a tall figure appeared in the doorway – Nanny!

Fifty-one

She was a stately woman of middle years, taller than Mungo, but on eye-level with Abena. Her high cheekbones, broad lips and strong chin spoke of a woman of authority. On the lower part of her cheeks, from ear to mouth, were two parallel scars. She was wearing a white headscarf and a plain white linen smock down to her ankles. Contrary to what they'd heard, her only adornment was a red necklace of dried beads the size of acorns. No human teeth. No dried ears or noses. No trophies of the Red Coats.

Nanny held herself as straight as a bean-pole while staring at each or them in turn. Her jet-black eyes seemed to bore into their souls. They softened slightly on seeing Abena's wounds. Her suffering at white hands was painfully apparent.

From the African girl, the *obeah* turned her glare on the scrawny, pasty-faced, ginger boy. Her eyes narrowed to two slits.

'What sort of *baccara* are you?' she snarled. 'A spy?'

Mungo was about to object, when Abena squeezed his arm.

'Oh no-o-o!' she said in a low growl.

In her own tongue she continued, 'This boy was

brought to Jamaica and sold as a domestic slave. I can vouch for that. Without him, I would be dead and none of us would have made it to safety.'

Nanny snorted.

'You are safe, thanks to my soldiers!'

Abena saw the hatred in her eyes as she stared Mungo up and down. Finally, she spat on the ground.

'Whites aren't to be trusted! They never keep their word. He must be sent back to his own kind!'

Abena suddenly exploded into a burst of words that took the woman aback. Her blazing eyes told Mungo she was speaking up on his behalf. Only afterwards did he learn what she had said – how he'd saved her life and helped her escape. When that had no effect – for Nanny hated all whites – she changed tactics. Abena said she was an *obeah* too: she could call up the spirits, turn herself into a crow or locust – or even worse. Did Nanny want to pit her powers against Abena's?

For good measure, she also told Nanny of the sketch, how it could be valuable to them – if the rebel leader could get it to a white abolitionist.

The girl's impassioned voice, one moment gruff and menacing, the next mellow and beguiling, sowed seeds of doubt in the older woman's mind. There was a long, tense silence. Nanny's eyes moved back and forth from the girl to Mungo as she was making up her mind.

Finally, her glare came to rest on the boy's bright red hair. Inquisitively, her long brown fingers pulled at a ginger tuft. Whether she expected to burn her hand or brush off red dust wasn't certain. When neither happened, she was puzzled.

Abena seized her opportunity.

'Red hair is lucky: it acts as a magic charm in battle, deflecting enemy bullets and weapons. If you had Mungo in your army, he'd bring you good luck.'

Nanny pushed her fingers through the thick bush of red hair, muttering, 'Mmmm... A red-haired rebel could confuse a *baccara* party...'

Abruptly, she barked orders to the waiting group.

'Take the girl to hospital and see to her wounds. Find a place in the men's hut for the boy. I'll decide his fate tomorrow.'

While Abena was led away in one direction, Mungo was taken to a wooden cabin at the far end of the village. The man who provided him with a sleeping mat introduced himself as Tackie; the young woman who brought food was Afua.

When Mungo asked about names, Tackie explained, 'We try to restore our lost African homeland, but we also add what's useful from our new world. So we keep our African names, but speak English as a common tongue.'

While he was talking, Mungo tucked into a hot meal of sweet potatoes, beans, fish and corn on the cob.

'Most of us come from the Gold Coast,' Tackie continued, 'but from different tribes – Ibo, Fanti,

Ashanti, Akin, Guinean. To avoid disagreement, we try to establish new ties so that everyone gets on with each other.'

Mungo smacked his lips: the food and drink were good. They were served in clay pots and hollowed-out gourds. In the gloom of the hut, light came from long tapered candles. Seeing his surprise, Afua told him, 'We make our own candles out of fat and oil, and we get wax and honey from wild bees. Women grow the crops – potatoes, yams, squash, beans, some maize and rice, often what we were used to back home, while men do the hunting – wild boar, and fish and turtles in the sea at the foot of John Crow Mountains. We even make butter from the fat of palm tree worms and peanuts. Very tasty.'

Mungo screwed up his nose as he asked, 'What about guns and tools? You don't make those, do you?'

'Oh no,' said Tackie. 'We buy and sell at market: our barbecued game and fish in exchange for cloth, medicine, guns and tools. Townspeople ask no questions; they're glad to trade.'

Afua laughed, adding, 'We have other means, too. If English soldiers come too close, we relieve them of their guns; and now and then we raid a plantation, though we try not to harm anyone.'

'Guns and ammunition are what we lack most,' said Tackie.

'What happens if you're caught?' enquired Mungo.

'We're burnt at the stake, heads chopped off, broken on the rack... We're a proud people. Some of us, like Nanny, were born free. We'd rather be tortured to death than become slaves.'

Mungo was exhausted after the long trek. It was long after dawn when he woke up. A messenger had come for Mungo: Nanny had made her decision, and the boy was led off to learn his fate.

The *obeah* woman was waiting for him outside her hut, her brows puckered in a scowl. She ordered Mungo to sit in the dust while she pronounced her verdict.

'The trackers say a hundred-strong force has been despatched from England to root us out. They're planning to catch us unawares by creeping up from the rear, landing at Port Antonio and Hope Bay. So be it. We'll be ready!'

She looked at him with the hint of a contemptuous smile on her lips. 'And you, boy, will act as decoy. You will lure the Red Coats into an ambush.'

Mungo nodded slowly, uncertain whether he was being set up for soldiers to take pot shots at. Since he might be going to his death, he asked a bold question.

'Can't you use your magic against the English?'

Her black eyes narrowed and she hissed mysteriously,

'Oh yes-ss. My warriors wear amulets to protect them from injury and our rituals weaken the enemy before battle. I'll use all the magic I can.'

She sighed. 'Sometimes, however, magic isn't enough, especially when the *baccara* sneak up from behind.'

'I see,' said Mungo (though he didn't).

'Go now, we must prepare for battle. Tonight we shall sing and dance to give us strength and cunning.'

Someone was waiting in the hut when he went back. At first, blinded by the sudden change from bright sunshine to darkness, he didn't notice the figure squatting in the shadows. It was only as he got stuck into a cold breakfast of boiled rice and bananas, that he heard a rustle behind him.

'Who's there?' he cried, remembering the deadly snake in the cave.

A low rumble like distant thunder announced the visitor's presence.

'Just an old bag of bones.'

Mungo couldn't believe his ears. He dropped the banana leaf spoon, jumped up and hugged his old friend.

'Mr Kwasi! How on earth? We thought you...'

'You don't get rid of me that easily,' Kwasi said with a chuckle. 'Old Kwasi's made of tough teak, not ash.'

He told Mungo how, after leading their pursuers

astray, he'd hidden in a pool, breathing through a hollow reed as he lay submerged. They had searched everywhere without finding him. Only afterwards did he discover he had crocodiles for company in the pool!

'...but they didn't seem to fancy my tough old flesh!'

They both laughed with relief.

'Tell me what Nanny said,' muttered the old man. When Mungo told him, Kwasi retorted, 'Good. While you were out, a woman, Amele, came to say they were transferring Abena to a special women's village at Guy's Town. She'll be in good hands there; they'll look after her wounds.'

After breakfast Mungo took a walk about the village, keeping inside the stockade. What struck him about the free Africans was their look of confidence and self-respect; they seemed to walk taller than the slaves he'd known, and they smiled and laughed freely.

Kwasi and Mungo were invited at dusk to a great clearing outside Nanny's hut. Squatting under an awning were musicians: two with conch shells, two with cow horns, five with different-sized drums made out of hollowed tree trunks and hog hide, and one with a long bamboo pole from which he was blowing bass notes.

Never before in his life had Mungo seen or heard such singing and dancing, such grace and wit as the women and men whirled about the dusty clearing.

Everyone joined in, clapping their hands in time with the dance and singing songs in a strange tongue – tunes their ancestors must have sung.

No one danced more vigorously than Nanny. For the dance she'd donned her gruesome ankle and neck bracelets, and strung a girdle of knives about her waist. She seemed to be acting out a battle, thrusting with an imaginary spear, firing arrows, wrestling with invisible enemies. Her feet barely touched the ground. Just to watch her made Mungo dizzy.

The dancing went on well into the night, fuelled by calabashes of palm wine. Kwasi and Mungo made their excuses early and trudged off to their bed mats.

'Tomorrow you march off to fight the foe, your own white people,' said the old man. 'Nanny reckons your ginger mop is a magic charm!'

Mungo objected, 'Those whites are as much my own as the blacks who sold you into slavery. This isn't about black against white – it's masters against freedom-fighters.'

Then he added, 'No one ever called my ginger hair a magic charm before!'

He gave a tired yawn, A few moments later he called out sleepily:

'Mr Kwasi?'

'Yes?'

'We made it!'

Fifty-two

Early next morning, Mungo became Private Mungo in the rebel army. As in any army, he had to take an oath of allegiance before he could enlist. Not to the King. Not to the Governor of Jamaica. Not to God. But to 'The Community of Free People of Jamaica'.

Along with other recruits, he was taken to the top of Pumpkin Hill and instructed to repeat the following:

> *I do solemnly swear to fight English raiding parties to the death.*
>
> *I do pledge allegiance to the Community of Free People of Jamaica, acknowledging that the island belongs to all who live in it, black and white; that all have the right to live forever in a perfect state of freedom and liberty.*

I can swear to that with a clear conscience, he told himself with a smile.

When the war party of some thirty men and women was assembled, Nanny led them off, singing, beyond the stockade. On the way they picked up other groups, until close on seventy soldiers were marching behind the leader. Last to join was a band of twenty led by the colourful hunchback who had saved Mungo and Abena. He was Nanny's brother, Quao.

It soon became plain to Mungo, however, that this rag-taggle band of men, women and children might have the upper hand in enthusiasm, but they lacked the real tools of war. They were up against experienced, professional, well-armed soldiers of the King.

The rebel leader herself was armed with nothing more than old knives – like most of her followers. Only a dozen carried muskets or any other firearm. Most had nothing more threatening than wooden clubs, home-made spears, machetes and digging tools. Such weapons would be useful in hand-to-hand combat – but first they had to get past enemy guns.

A young fellow-recruit kept Mungo company at the rear as the column snaked its way along half-hidden paths through rough terrain.

He introduced himself. 'I'm Kwaku. Have you seen battle before?'

Mungo shook his head. 'And you?'

'Only as shouter.'

'What's a shouter?'

'Boys who creep as close as they can to an enemy patrol and shout: 'Come, *baccara*. Come, *baccara*!' Then they run away as fast as they can, and lead the soldiers into an ambush.'

He giggled, showing his strong white teeth.

'But this is more exciting. I might get to kill a soldier.'

'Do you really think so?' asked Mungo, wondering whether Kwaku's zeal was based on mere bravado.

The black boy twirled his bamboo lance as he chewed on the question. Then he said soberly in a grown-up voice, 'We shouldn't underestimate the enemy. He has superior fire-power. What do we have? A few old guns and hardly any powder. For shot we've mainly pebbles, coins, buttons – whatever fits the breach. So what can we do about it?'

He answered his own question. 'Take guns from the enemy!'

Mungo laughed.

'We have to avoid their bullets first.'

'We can!'

'How can you be so sure?'

'Nanny has magic powers. When the soldiers fire, she pulls up her skirts and bares her backside. Then she catches the bullets in her bottom and fires them back at the soldiers.'

Mungo laughed.

'...And kills them all stone dead, I suppose.'

Kwaku laughed too.

'Well, she's got other tricks up her skirts.'

'Such as?' asked Mungo, expecting more rude tales of Nanny's backside.

'She's brilliant at bush fighting. That's where the English are at a disadvantage. They're used to an open battlefield with lots of room to make charges down the flanks. So she lures them into the bush and forces them to walk in single file along narrow pathways. And they march along in their scarlet uniforms, as bold as brass, beating their drum – dead easy to spot and pick off.'

'I hope you're right,' said Mungo doubtfully.

All day long Nanny's troops marched northwards, stopping only at rebel settlements for rest and refreshment. They stayed the night at Guy's Town – a special *polinck* or camp for children, sick women and mothers-to-be.

Mungo took the opportunity to seek out Abena, taking Kwaku along as interpreter. He found her in a long, airy hut containing rows of wooden beds and straw mattresses. Women who'd recently had babies filled most of the beds, while Abena was at the far end, behind a bamboo screen .

She was half-asleep, no doubt sedated by herbal potions. Her torn ear and what could be seen of her arms and back were covered in ointment and fresh herbs.

'How do you feel?' asked Mungo, touching her hand.

She just blinked, as if to say: not bad, not good.

He looked with pity at the once-spirited girl, now barely able to open her eyes or move her limbs. What a superhuman effort she'd made to get this far! Was it all to be in vain? Would her strength and spirit give out?

So near and yet so far…

'I'm a soldier now,' he said, with a reassuring smile, 'a secret weapon to defeat the foe. Nanny reckons my hair's like a red rag to a bull. I'll entice the enemy into an ambush. After we've won, Nanny'll probably make me a colonel or general…'

He babbled on to fill the empty space as she closed her eyes, unable or unwilling to talk.

'She'll be fine,' broke in an old woman. 'She needs lots of peace and quiet. So shoo-oo.'

The two young recruits left the hospital thinking the same thoughts. Peace and quiet were the last things Abena would get if they didn't stop the Red Coats. The English would set fire to every village they came upon, killing each man, woman and child.

That night, before Mungo had a chance to sleep, he was summoned to Nanny's quarters, where half a dozen of her lieutenants were already assembled. She didn't detain him – just long enough to give him orders.

'I'm giving you a dangerous mission.'

He was both nervous and proud to hear these words. 'Dangerous' meant he might die – killed by his own white people. But he was proud to be entrusted with a mission by the black leader against white soldiers.

She spelled it out.

'Success depends on a cool head.'

She fixed him with a stare.

'Are you up to it?'

'Yes, Commander!' he replied firmly.

'All right,' she said with a tired sigh. 'Dismissed.'

Mungo was glad to have some rest at last, in a cramped compound with twenty or so men.

At the crack of dawn, an *abeng* provided the army's wake-up call and again they were on the move. Once more they climbed up and down wooded hills, pushed through trees and thick undergrowth, all the while following a narrow track. On the way they passed a deserted camp of huts in a valley criss-crossed by a fast-flowing river. All about them, sheer cliffs towered high above the empty town.

It was midday, unbearably hot and humid. To Mungo's relief, the command came to fall out. Immediately he plunged into the river to cool off. But the respite was short-lived, for he and about thirty others, including Kwaku and other shouters, were detailed for a further march – this time up the face of the far cliff.

As they started the climb, Mungo noticed that most of the soldiers were carrying guns; he and the shouters weren't.

Fifty-three

It took two hours to scale the cliff. At the top, even the indefatigable Nanny was out of breath.

'Fall out,' she ordered. 'Take a break.'

As she was speaking, the sound of drums came from the hills around, and a distant *abeng* trumpeted a long, low, single note.

'The look-outs have sighted enemy movement,' explained an older man called Kojo, 'about five or six miles away, by the sound of it.'

Nanny stood up and listened intently as more drumming echoed round the hills. She smiled to herself as if all was going to plan. Advancing across the flat ridge, she fell to her knees, praying to the spirits for help in the coming encounter. Her movements disturbed a pigeon which fluttered up into the sky.

Mungo heard a sigh of wonder rise from the watching men, as if the bird was Nanny's spirit flying off to spy on the enemy. When, five minutes later, the pigeon returned to settle in a tamarind tree, they had no doubt that the bird possessed vital information to ensure victory.

When the party set off again, Nanny strode out confidently, brushing aside vine and bramble, bush and branch, setting turkey vultures and bush pigs to flight. Now and again, a distant drum resounded and, after a while, it was joined by another – this one beating out quite a different, harsher rhythm: *rat-tat-tat-tat, rat-tat-tat-tat!*

Nanny held up her hand.

Kojo whispered in Mungo's ear,

'The Red Coat drum.'

The rebel soldiers knew their orders and, at a wave from Nanny, spread out on either side of the track, concealing themselves in the bushes. The dusky colour of their skin and their grey-green tunics blended well into the undergrowth. Meanwhile, Nanny led Mungo forward to a palm-encircled clearing where he could look down on the cockpits behind and ahead.

A tense silence had fallen over the narrow pathway. Nothing stirred except huge-winged, circling vultures looking down hungrily at the intruders. What game of hide-and-seek was this? Why were big black crows crouching behind bushes? Why was the orange-crested cockatoo standing alone in the open? What was the distant flock of redbreasts?

First it was the shouters' turn to go into battle. With a wave to Mungo, Kwaku dashed off down the path with two other boys. It wasn't hard for them to locate the enemy. Their task was to entice the soldiers along the path leading to the clearing where Mungo lay in wait. To do so, they had to jump out from behind a bush or tree, call *'Baccara!'* to taunt them, then scuttle back as fast as their legs could carry them. Hopefully, by the time the Red Coats raised their guns, they'd be out of harm's way.

All seemed to be going to plan. Mungo heard high-pitched yells – *'Baccara! Baccara! Baccara!'* and the sudden staccato shouts of officers – 'There, over there. Fire! fire! fire!'

Then came a series of bangs and clouds of gunsmoke rising above the trees, followed by loud curses as the army's quarry disappeared.

But something must have gone wrong because, at the third alarm, a sharp shriek rang out, followed by a tense silence, then a further volley of shots and a second scream. Amid the hubbub of voices from unseen soldiers, Mungo heard someone shout, 'That'll teach the little beggars!'

Several minutes later, a single boy came running into the clearing, all out of breath.

'Afu tripped and fell... They shot him... Kwaku tried to pull him clear, but he was shot too.'

Nanny showed no sign of emotion.

'Never mind, you achieved your purpose,' she said.

Poor Kwaku, thought Mungo. He never did get to shoot a soldier.

He didn't have long to dwell on his friend's fate: the incessant *rat-tat-tat-tat* was coming closer and closer and he could tell by the numbers of birds starting up from the bush that enemy soldiers were approaching his forward position.

The boy's heart was beating fast. Thoughts of Abena and Kwasi helped steel him for the coming ordeal; yet they couldn't prevent his hands shaking or the hairs on his neck springing up like porcupine quills. Beside the drums, he could hear the stamp of feet, muffled curses and occasional rapped orders. The soldiers were coming closer by the minute.

All at once, the bushes parted and a lanky officer, sweating heavily, led a long line of dusty, musket-bearing Red Coats into the clearing. Behind them came a score or more of black baggage-carriers. The officer's neck swivelled in all directions, like an alert night owl.

Spotting the pale-faced, ginger boy sitting on a tussock, the officer suddenly halted in his tracks. This was the last thing he expected. Fearing a trap, he signalled troops to spread out right and left, covering the lone figure with their guns. From the edge of the clearing, he shouted uncertainly, 'Who goes there? Friend or foe?'

'Friend!' Mungo called back just as nervously.

'What are you doing in bandit country?'

This last question was put as the officer stepped warily towards the boy, rifle cocked.

'I was captured, sir… Bush Rebels… I escaped!'

The officer rapped an order.

'Lieutenant Tudor! Search that man thoroughly.'

Mungo was frisked from top to toe. It was evident he was unarmed. But the officer was still suspicious. It was hard to credit that a white boy would be siding with blacks. Yet what else could he be doing there?

'How did you escape?'

'I was locked up in a rebel *polinck*, sir, about an hour's march from here. When the savages got drunk on palm wine, I stole away. I was making for the coast.'

The Captain's eyes narrowed. This boy could be of use as a scout.

'Could you take us to the *polinck?*'

Mungo shook his head.

'I'd like to, sir, but I'm heading for Port Antonio.'

The officer was clearly irritated.

'We'll take you to Port Antonio ourselves – once we've cleaned out the rebel stronghold.'

Mungo was about to object, but swallowed his words as the officer jabbed a musket into the small of his back.

'You'll obey King's orders, boy!'

Mungo shrugged, as if it was all the same to him.

'Well, I do know the way to their town – but it's down a steep slope into a valley crossed by a river.'

'Lead on, boy. My men are hot and tired. They're badly in need of a drink. Get going!'

Nanny's plan was working a treat.

With Mungo's ginger mop bobbing up and down

in front, the soldiers followed, single-file, along the narrow defile through dense bush. The track twisted and turned so frequently, the soldiers at front and rear never had a full view of their comrades.

All at once, a shot rang out. It was hard to tell where it came from. But a Red Coat fell to the ground, clutching his chest.

'Open fire!' yelled the officer in the vanguard.

Desperately, soldiers searched the bushes for wisps of gunsmoke. But no sooner was smoke spotted than a volley rang out from the other side – and two more soldiers bit the dust.

The column halted in its tracks, undecided whether to retreat or proceed. While they were hesitating, the two back markers vanished, along with their muskets.

Captain Soaper made a snap decision.

'Forward, men, at a trot. Fire at will.'

The hidden enemy, fresh and wise to forest ways, simply melted away like gunsmoke before the Red Coats had reloaded.

The commander's suspicions now grew. Had the boy deliberately led them into an ambush? Mungo knew his life hung by a thread. The rebels must have realised that too for, apart from stragglers disappearing without a sound, no more shots were fired.

Luckily for Mungo, the column soon reached the precipice overlooking the 'rebel town'. By now it was eight o'clock and fast growing dark. Once again

Captain Soaper was faced with a dilemma. Should he chance the steep descent or should he strike camp in the open, in sight of the inviting river? When he inspected his men, he found that not only had he lost a dozen soldiers, but the black baggage-carriers had all fled – along with tents and equipment.

He had no choice but to consult Mungo.

'Are you sure there are no rebels down there?'

'Yes, sir, mostly women and *piccaninnies* – no danger.'

Advancing to the edge of the cliff, the officer put his telescope to one eye and dimly made out about a hundred women and children scrambling up the hill opposite. Aware of the enemy approach, they were laden down with whatever they could save.

'Men,' shouted the commander, 'give them a taste of English buckshot!'

The fleeing women and children were too far away for accurate fire. But as a row of kneeling riflemen let off a volley into the thick of the fleeing crowd, Mungo saw a few sway and fall: they either remained where they fell or were helped up, and went on up the hill. There was little the boy could do, but he made an attempt.

'We should hurry, sir, while it's still light.'

That spurred the Captain into a burst of orders.

'Cease fire! Form up! Single File! Prepare for descent!'

Mungo led the soldiers down the cliff path into the valley below. To their relief, they reached the bottom unmolested. It was only when they entered the town that they realised why. It was deserted. Not a soul remained. The place appeared safe enough for the soldiers to make their quarters in the wooden shacks.

Before bedding down, however, they refreshed themselves in the cool stream and cooked the food they'd salvaged from knapsacks left by the baggage-carriers. The soldiers were so exhausted after their long march that, with just two sentries posted, they retired to the huts, glad of a good night's sleep.

Mungo was given bed space in the officers' hut.

He realised he was in a strange situation. Because he was white, the officers treated him as one of their own, and he felt a bit sorry to be betraying them. Yet when he thought of what Kwasi, Abena and other slaves had been through, he knew that skin colour was irrelevant. What counted was what was right!

'Tomorrow I'll lead you to Nanny Town,' he promised the officers.

Fifty-four

No sooner did Mungo hear the snores of Captain Soaper and Major Ashworth, than he quietly slipped out of the hut and melted away into the darkness. As arranged, he met up with the waiting rebels hiding in the bush just a stone's throw away.

'You did well, boy!' muttered Nanny.

Praise indeed, thought Mungo!

Now for the next phase of Nanny's plan. As the soldiers slept, a group of warriors crawled as close as they dared to the huts and threw strips of lightning wood on to the thatched roofs.

Almost immediately the thatch began to smoulder, then burst into flame. It wasn't long before the entire camp was ablaze and, as the huts burned, the soldiers rushed out in confusion, leaving boots, rifles and ammunition behind.

This was the signal for rebels to swarm through the burning huts, salvaging firearms, gunpowder and shot, as the soldiers stumbled into the darkness.

For the first time, Nanny's army had the upper hand in guns and ammunition.

The panic-stricken, half-dressed Red Coats fled before their pursuers, splashing through the river and scrambling back up the steep hill. Nanny let them go. She had what she wanted; there was no point in provoking the Big White Chief across the seas into sending an even bigger force.

When dawn broke, the battlefield was littered with discarded boots, coats and firearms. A single straggler was found, an officer, lying in the river with a broken ankle.

'If you value your life,' Nanny threatened, 'you'll obey my orders. You will write a note, as I dictate.'

Once the man's leg was patched up, she handed him a palm-bark pen.

'I've no ink,' whined the man.

'Use blood!' ordered Nanny, running a knife along his forearm.

The English soldier had no choice. It was either his blood or his life. He wrote down what Nanny dictated:

Let the King know, we routed a hundred Red Coats.
We let them go unharmed.
Send more soldiers and we shall defeat them too.
We want peace, not war.
                    Nanny of Nanny's Town

When the officer was fit enough to walk, he was helped to a patrol route used by the militia and left to await rescue.

All the rebels could do now was wait. Hopefully,

the British would be forced to come to terms, leaving them in peace.

Several days later, Mungo was reunited with Kwasi and together they went to visit Abena. When he saw her empty bed, he feared the worst. A cold hand gripped his heart, forcing tears into his eyes and goose-pimples on his skin. Then a hoarse, cheery voice at once calmed him down.

She was up and about, chatting gaily to other women as if she were back in Africa. When she saw the old man and boy approach, a wide smile lit up her face. It was the first time Mungo noticed a lucky gap between her top front teeth.

'Good day, friends,' she called. 'How you are?'

Mungo grinned at her asking in English.

'How are you?'

'Me no good,' she responded, evidently proud of her progress in English.

Kwasi spared her by speaking their common tongue: he brought her up to date with events, including Mungo's contribution to victory.

To the boy's surprise, instead of congratulations, she flung a garbled mixture of words at him, accompanied by finger prods, head-shaking and arm-waving.

'Slaves... Engleesh... Ah-freeca... Shee-eep...'

Kwasi interpreted.

'She says whites aren't to be trusted. They'll agree to peace in word only, then sneak up and stab us in the back. We'll only be safe when all slaves are free.'

Mungo shook his head.

'That's as may be, but we can't defeat soldiers by words alone. Nor with sticks and stones and rusty old guns. We need allies. Not all whites are bad. Some are slaves like me. Some hate slavery.'

Kwasi turned to the girl, telling her Mungo's words, then adding his own. Finally, he pointed to the boy's chest, saying to him, 'I've heard talk of a white medicine man in Kingston. He and some of his followers – Methodists, they call themselves – are campaigning to put an end to slavery. If we can get Abena's sketch to him, he might use it as evidence to show how wrong the slave trade is, even by white laws.'

Mungo shrugged.

'Even if the sketch were to help, how are we to get it to him?'

Almost as soon as the words passed his lips, he realised whom Kwasi had in mind.

'Oh, no!'

'Oh, yes,' said Kwasi. 'You're our only hope. You've brought it so far, you wouldn't want to waste it, would you?'

'We can't act without Nanny's say-so,' Mungo muttered, half-hoping the formidable priestess would say no.

But she readily consented.

'You've proved your worth, white boy,' she growled.

'Now you can help in an even greater cause: freedom for all slaves, black and white.'

When Nanny's followers learned of Mungo's mission, they arranged a grand send-off for him. The highlight of the celebrations was the cleansing ritual: Nanny danced about him, spraying him with a fly-whisk which she dipped into a gourd of magic water.

Abena and Kwasi looked on in amusement as the bedraggled boy, his wet hair the colour of burned cane, stood helplessly in the middle of the clearing, like a scarecrow in a cornfield. He didn't know whether to laugh or cry. In front of Abena he tried to put on a brave face.

The ceremony over, Nanny said, for all to hear:

'Go, rebel boy. Tell the White Medicine Man this: no white man can be truly free until every black man is free.'

Clutching the precious sketch to his chest, Mungo bade farewell to his closest friends, unsure whether he'd ever see them again.

He looked fondly at his first black friend in Jamaica and saw his missing ears, fingers and toes – the price of wanting to be free.

He gazed fondly at his second black friend and recalled the torture she'd endured – the price of wanting to be free. And he remembered vividly her brother's sad brown eyes.

'I'll do my best,' he promised.

As he turned away, the old man pressed something into his hand. It was his precious cock feathers.

'No, no,' Mungo began. But the tears in Kwasi's eyes told him he couldn't refuse. They were the old man's only possessions.

Abena accompanied him to the bush track, taking his hand in hers. As they parted, she gave him a brief hug, saying, 'Find mother, sister.' Sorrow filled her eyes; she reminded Mungo of her brother.

'I'll do what I can,' he said.

Pushing him away, Abena cried,

'Now, red monkey, shift yer arse!'

'Thank you,' Mungo said with a grin. 'I love you too.'

With that, he turned his back on one world and set off into another, seeking to make the two one.

Afterword

It was to be another eighty years before the British Parliament abolished the slave trade in 1807, and well over a hundred years before the Slavery Abolition Act outlawed slavery in the British colonies – though British slave ships continued to defy the law until the late 1860s. By then, at least fifteen million Africans and an unknown number of Europeans had crossed the Atlantic to become slaves in the Caribbean and in North and South America. The slave trade is estimated to have caused the deaths of some thirty to forty million more in slave raids and in the *barracoons.*

Everywhere they went, slaves fought for their freedom. In Hispaniola (now Haiti) they overthrew their white masters in the late eighteenth century, and set up an independent state.

The Bush Rebels of Jamaica continued to fight to defend their liberty. They suffered many defeats and setbacks at the hands of the militia and of the English soldiers sent to suppress them. Yet communities of free slaves, known as Maroons, survived. To this day, Maroon descendants still live in the Blue Mountains of Jamaica, intensely proud of their rebellious history and of leaders such as Nanny.

And eventually... some children of children of children did return to see their ancestral homes again. They did go back to Africa. In 2002 Beaula McCalla, who wrote the Foreword to this book, visited her ancestral home and eight blood relatives on the island of Bioko in Equatorial Guinea. Her homecoming was shown as a television documentary, *Motherland: A Genetic Journey*. It was a wonderful, heart-rending, painful, inspiring spiritual journey.

JAMES RIORDAN's first children's novel,
Sweet Clarinet, was shortlisted for the Whitbread Prize
in 1998 and won the NASEN award in 1999.
Match of Death won the Scottish Book Award in 2002.
His first picture-book for Frances Lincoln was
The Coming of Night, followed by *The Twelve Labours
of Hercules*, winner of a UK Reading Association
Award 1998, and *Jason and the Golden Fleece*.
James lives with his cat Tilly
in Portsmouth, Hampshire.

MIXING IT
Rosemary Hayes

Fatimah is a devout Muslim. Steve is a regular guy
who has never given much thought to faith.
Both happen to be in the same street the day
a terrorist bomb explodes. Steve is badly injured
and when the emergency services arrive,
Fatimah has bandaged his shattered leg and is
cradling his head in her lap, willing him to stay alive.
But the Press is there too, and their picture
makes the front page of every newspaper.
'Love across the divide,' scream the headlines.
Then the anonymous 'phone calls start.
Can Steve and Fatimah rise above the hatred
and learn to understand each other?
But while they are breaking down barriers,
the terrorists have another target in mind...

ISBN: 978-1-84507-495-1

GHADDAR THE GHOUL
and other Palestinian Stories
Sonia Nimr
Introduction by Ghada Karmi
Illustrated by Hannah Shaw

Why do Snakes eat Frogs?
What makes a Ghoul turn Vegetarian?
How can a Woman make a Bored Prince Smile?
The answers can be found in this
delicious anthology of Palestinian folk stories.
A wry sense of humour runs through their cast
of characterful women, genial tricksters
and mischievous animals.
Sonia Nimr's upbeat storytelling,
bubbling with wit and humour,
will delight readers discovering
for the first time the rich tradition
of Palestinian storytelling.

ISBN: 978-1-84507-523-1

**THE PRINCE WHO THOUGHT
HE WAS A ROOSTER**
and other Jewish Stories
Ann Jungman
Introduction by Michael Rosen
Illustrated by Sarah Adams

A Chilli Champion?... a Golem?...
a Prince who thinks he's a Rooster?
Find them all in this collection of traditional
Jewish tales – lovingly treasured, retold and carried
through countries as far apart as Poland, Tunisia,
Czechoslovakia, Morocco, Russia and Germany,
with a cast of eccentric princes, flustered tailors,
wise rabbis and the oldest champion of all!
Seasoned with wit, humour and magic,
Ann Jungman's retellings of stories familiar
to Jewish readers are sure to delight
a new, wider readership.

ISBN: 978-1-84507-794-5

GIVE ME SHELTER
Stories about children seeking asylum
Edited by Tony Bradman

Sabine is escaping a civil war...
Danny doesn't want to be soldier...
What has happened to Samir's family?

Here is a collection of stories about children
from all over the world who must leave their homes
and families behind to seek a new life in
a strange land. Many are escaping war
or persecution. All must become asylum seekers
in the free lands of the West.
If they do not escape, they will not survive.

These stories, some written by asylum seekers
and people who work closely with them,
tell the story of our humanity and the fight for
the most basic of our rights – to live.
It is a testimony to all the people in need of shelter
and those from safer countries who
act with sympathy and understanding.

ISBN: 978-1-84507-522-4

LINES IN THE SAND
New Writing on War and Peace
Edited by Mary Hoffman and Rhiannon Lassiter

Talented writers and illustrators from all over
the world have come together to produce this book.
They were inspired by their feelings about the conflict
in Iraq, though the wars covered in this collection
range from a 13th-century Crusade through
the earlier wars of the 20th century to recent
conflicts in Nigeria, the Falklands, Kosovo
and South Africa, right up to what
was happening in Iraq in 2003.

With over one hundred and fifty poems, stories
and pictures about war and peace,
Lines in the Sand offers hope for the future.

All profits and royalties to UNICEF

ISBN: 978-0-7112-2282-3